"Michelle Miller's writing hit
a zen master -- sudden, brutal ,
that don't just walk the razor's ____ they dance down it. And
though the people who inhabit them sometimes fall, the writer
never does. There is an old hotel in a ghost town, and its name
is the title of this book. When you check in, leave behind
everything you thought you understood about women, men and the
way they relate. Then let Miller show you around. You may not
want the same baggage when you leave. "

-- **Scott Nicolay,** writer, publisher
YOO-HOO Press, Farmington, NM

"With wry tenderness, Michelle Miller examines men, women,and
their efforts at loving. Paramount in Miller's characters is wonder
at the capricious quality of sexuality. In this era of questionable
gender roles, they approach the primitive Dance with chagrin and
hope. The goal is to penetrate, smash or at least understand the
barrier which keeps lover from lover, individuality from
communion, and the self from disillusion. Luminous in rage,
roughly sensual, pensive and bewildered, Miller's men and women
stalk each other in search of themselves. "

-- **J. Dianne Duff,** writer, co-editor
THE SPIRIT THAT WANTS ME

"A young woman seeks sanctuary in a ghost town to wrestle with
her conflicts and confusion about relationships, sexuality and her
need for other people. In solitude, the same conflicts, phantom-
like, continue to confront her. The poetic, ethereal images of
Hunger in the First Person Singular aptly portray the ambiguity
and ultimate indivisibility of our inner and external realities,
particularly in the realm of the romantic relationships with which
contemporary culture seems to struggle so much. "

-- **Jon Maaske, Ph.D.**
Clinical Psychologist, Samaritan Center of Albuquerque
and Trainee, Analyst Training Program,
C. G. Jung Institute of Santa Fe

"You may never have known such people as Michelle Miller writes about, or you may, in some aspects of your life, be one of them. Her characters live, or try to live, their own lives, to follow and satisfy their own desires in the face of society's never-ending attempt to turn them (and all of us, for that matter) into 'normal, ordinary human beings.' How they cope, or try to cope, is strikingly different. I would especially recommend this book to men. Miller is a truly liberated human being, a writer who understands that both women and men have been deeply wounded by the world in which we live. Her compassion for us all transcends gender."

-- **Chuck Cockelreas,** writer, editor,
Men's Wellness Advocate

*"The ambivalence of heart-mind relationships and the relentless struggle of the spirit evolving toward liberation are themes wholly and eloquently embraced in this volume. The communication tools of imagery and text become **One** so completely, it is no surprise to learn the two creative souls responsible for them (Michelle Miller and Jude Catallo) go back a very long way together. A shared vision of Power, Vulnerability and **Process** emerges.*

*"Conscious readers of this book will recognize Miller's hunger. We will feel its gnawing in Catallo's **Nomads** and make eye contact with it in her **Refuge**. At certain moments we will be victims; at other times, victors. But we will not be mere bystanders as we travel these pages. Catallo's images and Miller's words prohibit it. Instead, we are offered a 'script without dialogue' which will help us to confront our respective ghosts and angels with more hope and courage."*

-- **Jill Kiefer**, writer, co-editor
THE SPIRIT THAT WANTS ME

HUNGER IN THE

FIRST PERSON SINGULAR

Stories of Desire and Power

Michelle Miller

Printed in the United States of America
        First Printing, 1992
        ISBN 0-938513-15-X
        L.I.C.# 92-72299

An earlier version of "Water Rites" appears in
The Spirit That Wants Me: a New Mexico Anthology.

AMADOR PUBLISHERS
P. O. Box 12335
Albuquerque, NM 87195 USA

Acknowledgments go to Studio Village Writers Workshop and others who read and critiqued various drafts of this fiction, including Carol Berge, Chuck Cockelreas, Jim Burbank, Sharon Niederman, Carl Ginsburg, Jill Kiefer, J. Dianne Duff, Janet Maher and Rob Cohen. Thanks to Isaac Chocrón, Harry Willson and Adela Amador for their faith and invaluable editorial advice. Particular thanks to sister Jude and fellow creatives Dianne, Jill, Funk, Sal, Suzy, Virgie, Stephanie and Wade for their encouragement, feedback, friendship & survival support during the living and the writing. Final thanks to: Catherine who proofread, Katie who listened, Peggy who waited for a book, Cat who gave permission, Brad who lent me his compass, my family and the woman at the door.

For all my angels and ghosts.

AUTHOR: Michelle Miller is a writer and playwright living in Albuquerque, New Mexico. Her poetry, short fiction and articles have appeared in various literary & arts magazines in the U.S. and Canada, including *Prism International, Island, Center, Artspace, Women Artists and Writers of the Southwest,* and *Pudding.* In the 1980s Miller was a member of New Mexico's poetry performance trio, Lit Dog Triad. Four of Miller's plays (*The Bonsai Garden, Spiderplay, The Vintage Erotica Reading Room,* and *The Eden Vent*) have been produced at the University of New Mexico's Rodey Theatre. *The Eden Vent* was awarded a Fall 1992 production at New Mexico State University. Miller is Co-Editor with Jill Kiefer and Dianne Duff of *The Spirit That Wants Me,* a New Mexico Anthology.

ARTIST: Jude Catallo is an artist living on the edge of Lake Superior in Northern Michigan. Catallo studied print making in Louisiana and Michigan, and has exhibited in Louisiana, Massachusetts, Michigan and Colorado.

The juxtaposition of Catallo's images and Miller's words into this volume is the realization of a 26-year-old dream of best friends.

COVER LETTERING: Mark Lee Funk is an artist and writer living in Albuquerque, New Mexico.

COVER DESIGN: Claiborne O'Connor is an artist living in Albuquerque, New Mexico, proprietor of See O See Studios.

CONTENTS

HUNGER IN THE FIRST PERSON SINGULAR

II. STORIES OF DESIRE AND POWER

TABLE OF PLATES

ARTIST'S NOTE: Dry point, like etching, is an intaglio process by which the image is transferred from a recessed line in either a metal or lexan plate. In printing on a traditional press, the paper is forced down into the line. Editions are no greater than 25 per print, due to the evolving loss of details with each print rendered.

Introduction

Michelle Miller's volume of short fiction will be a pleasant surprise for people like myself who have known the writer's accomplished plays. The surprise heightens as these stories immerse us in a very private world, that of a woman unsatisfied with the relations she establishes and, even worse, with her behavior in them. Most ironically, this is a thinking, liberal, emancipated woman who, instead of enjoying her new liberty and rights, finds that these advantages create an oppressive force around her.

The woman in "Bonsai" struggles unsuccessfully to incorporate her hippie lover into her daily, conventional sort of intellectual living. The woman in the novella, *Hunger in the First Person Singular,* (aren't they the same woman?) has given up any kind of struggle and, like Thoreau in *Walden,* which she mentions, takes refuge in a ghost town where she writes what we read and where, instead of peace and serenity, she is haunted by her former life.

What this woman pursues is a pilgrimage to herself, with all that it connotes: the reader can immerse himself in her confession, almost making it his own, or he can keep detached, observing the idiosyncrasies of this woman who ran away.

The ghost town seems an ideal surrounding to her, a sort of paradise. Is it true or is it her hunger to be alone that makes it a paradise? Hunger that turns out to be the same hunger she experienced in the city, in "Bonsai," with the appearance of a man who could be real or imagined, a man who could be like the hippie or like the ideal, never to be attained.

So Michelle Miller's stories turn out to be a sort of novel; more than that, they are a diary or a journal that succeeds in exposing the dramatic and touching complexities of today's liberated woman.

-- Isaac Chocrón
Playwright, Novelist
Caracas, Venezuela
1992 PNM Endowed Chair,
University of New Mexico

"... when the two shall be one, and the outside as the inside, and the male with the female, neither male nor female. Now the two are one, when we speak truth among ourselves, and in two bodies there shall be one soul without dissimulation. "

circa A.D. 120-140
Attributed to Clement of Rome
"An Ancient Homily"

"It is clear that the psyche of each desires something else which it is unable to speak, but it prophesies what it desires and speaks in riddles. "

Plato, ***Symposium***
[Aristophanes]

" 'There is a space between us,' he said...
And she was as if magically aware of their being balanced in separation, in the boat.
'But I am very near,' she said caressively, gaily.
'Yet distant, distant,' he said.
'Yet we cannot very well change, whilst we are on the water...' "

Women in Love
D. H. Lawrence

HUNGER IN THE FIRST PERSON SINGULAR

1. Hunger

When I think back to why I was compelled to leave the world of people, the answers don't come easily. Not as easily as they came at the time, when I was overwhelmed with urgent anger and frustration. I came here for a healing, and in large part I have been healed -- enough so that it requires no small effort to summon the memory of why I took sanctuary.

I'm going to tell this in the first person singular. For too long now I have been in solitude, no company except my own voice, as papery white and brittle from disuse as a snakeskin left to fragment in this dusted wind. I no longer feel there is any purpose to writing in the voice of a fictitious persona, as I did in my novels, and I want to hear what I will say if I write from my unsophisticated center. This must be raw, first draft, my true voice, the one that hasn't yet spoken. There are no longer any other voices, for me. None of that "Introduce X, enter Y, confrontation, dismay, distrust, sudden passion, she gives in, he leaves." Not for a moment will I let myself think of this in the third person, not even for a brief outline.

That's what this place does. You lose a sense of

order; you create a new one. Your own. New rituals.
New calendars. Long ago I lost my sense of "real world"
time. I know when it's morning, noon, evening. I've lost
the months but I know the seasons, and I have a rough idea
of the years. Let's see -- I've been here four years? Four
years, I think.
When I think of what I'd have to do to get this story
out into civilization, I laugh. To publish this I would have
to change my whole life. Again. First I'd have to mail it
to my agent. Nearest post office is a several days' hike.
(My jeep is four days from here, but it doesn't run
anymore.)   All of that would require exposing my
whereabouts, or at least my existence.   I had one
moderately successful novel, but my second one -- about a
hermaphrodite -- only gathered a modest cult following.
Then I disappeared, and I'm sure the world has presumed
death, foul play. If I resurfaced now with manuscript in
hand, my publisher would grab it.   What a lot of
excitement it would create -- *NOVELIST RESURRECTED,
FROM GHOST TOWN!* It would be easy -- talk shows this
time, contracts, movie rights, even a market for my
remaindered books! Funny to think that, if I turned back
to it, I could have everything I left, multiplied. Society
rewards those who shun her, her rebels and hermits; we
make good copy.
    I begin to remember what it's like, back there. I
wonder, if I were in a car approaching, say, Chicago --
within thirty miles from the outskirts -- would my mind
begin that chant which became continual white noise, day
and night, awake or asleep? Schedules, plans, self-image,
things to buy, what to wear, money, time, motion,
thinking, feeding, hunger, money, motion...even after all
this time away, I suspect it would begin again, that soon.
Only, now that I know there is another way to be inside

one's self, I would struggle against it.

The first thing my ghost town solitude taught me was that for thirty-seven years of my life, with every movement, every breath, I had been playing a role. The role was Woman. Mysterious, exotic Woman, with all the implications, since Biblical times, of that word. I was all of it. I was Every Woman Every Man Has Ever Known or Dreamed of Knowing. I found out pretty early it's what's *not* there that men want -- to suffer, to chase, to never-quite-catch. If they do catch a woman, they want her to turn on them, to be unfaithful, to become a shrew, to somehow severely disappoint their ideal. Once I figured that out, I decided, of course, to play the elusive woman. Because the terrible truth was, I was always *there*. Totally accessible. Right in the moment, living every follicle, sucking up the air and touching to bruise. I called it love, but it was hunger.

The second lesson my ghost town taught me is that hunger is the only emotion. All the other "emotions" are simply hunger in different stages -- hunt, feed, satiation. I watched a baby rattlesnake one day as it crossed Main Street. Its head darted in seizures, sensitive to particles of air and motion on all sides. It spied a mouse and went completely still, so focused I could have walked past it with no ramifications. Being at some distance, I tested this. Before the mouse appeared, the snake had reacted to the vibration of my walking stick. I tapped now, while the snake stalked the mouse. No response. Just like sex. Loss of space and time.

In the world, I was hungry and I fed myself. Men didn't want a hungry woman, except briefly, during sex. Mostly they wanted what they call the "sensuous" woman. Odd word, "sensuous." Calls to mind a blonde suburban gourmand in white shorts, inhaling coffee beans in a

California market. But what the brief, dark bed really was about was -- lust? No, still too soft a word, implies not getting. Hunger is what they wanted in the brief, dark bed. But not what came with it. Not a totally hungry, all-the-time hungry woman. I learned to suppress my appetite and "be nice." To only let the animal out on call, to tuck her in carefully the rest of the time. Like most women in that world, it made me schizophrenic. A friend once house-sat for me and, as commentary on my confusions, displayed my silk lingerie catalogue next to my copy of *Sexual Politics* on the bedside table. Months later he mentioned having done that and waited for a laugh. I hadn't noticed.

The very first morning in my ghost town, I got up and looked for a mirror. Even before building a fire for coffee. I wondered, as I scrubbed a corner of the sticky brown vanity glass in my cabin, "Why do I need a mirror? Who's going to see me?" I had carried in more of the outside world than I cared to admit -- more than one night in a ghost town could undo. Something about "orderly house, orderly mind." Not just wanting to *look* good, all alone in my town -- (or was I secretly hoping that some lovely, bronze tourist would appear?) -- it was that I needed to look good in order to *feel* good. For the first week, I rose dutifully to the mirror, cold-creamed my face, brushed my hair, applied eye liner, blusher and lipstick. On the street I watched for my reflection in the filmy store windows.

One morning I woke up to the bottom of the cold cream jar. For a former Woman of Mystery, who used to furtively memorize her lover's jawline while he slept, then give him a quick morning kiss and briskly exit, makeup and persona carefully applied, this was An Important Moment. That's another thing I have noticed here. The most ordinary moments become historical events; I now celebrate Jar Bottom Day. Not the exact calendar date, but I do recall it was the same week the aspens by the stream began to turn yellow. The jar is one of those thick, cobalt blue, glass ones. I've put a candle in it which I only burn on my holiday, the day the aspens yellow, only for a few moments, so it will last. The holiday has almost lost its meaning now; it's so long ago that I stopped with the makeup, so long ago since I broke out all the Main Street store windows and made my peace with the fact that I was not an elusive woman. It's like celebrating the first day you ever used a tampon. Pretty silly stuff. But I do it, I go through it. A sense of ritual, a sense of history.

The irony is that, if I were to return to the world now, I really *would* be a mystery woman. I'd get all kinds of offers, a woman who went without (anything, everything) for four years. Silk, sushi, champagne, a man's fingers. (What a traitor the body is. Writing those words down, I felt a sharp, vaginal heat.) But I imagine the veneer of mystery would wear off pretty fast. There I would be, openly hungry. Again.

My first year here, I wasn't hungry. After the initial novelty, it was a relief to be away from humanity. From all those assaultive demands on my image. Not having to hold in my stomach, worry about my profile, touch up my hair.

But lately the hunger. Just a phase. Four year itch. Hence this writing. I can fantasize what I hunger for, yet control it, only let in what I want, and only on paper. I can call up ghosts in my ghost town. Sometimes I've half seen, out of the corner of my eye, someone -- felt eyes watching me -- felt another's body heat on the back of my hand.

Let's say someone were to walk into my ghost town

right now, walk up to me sitting here at this old table in
front of the general store, where I am writing on these
large sheets off a roll of butcher paper with a couple of
pencils I sharpened with my knife. The paper is cobwebby
at the edges, water stained, permeated with the dust and
mildew scent of the old store. If someone saw me sitting
here, what would they see? I don't really know; it's been
four years since I've looked in a mirror.

. . .old habits. For a moment there, I was tempted to
step out of the first person and do one of those "he saw
her" scenes. I'd be describing what some fantasy of mine
would see in me, and I did make that one rule from the beginning, to speak what *I* know. So, describing myself from
the top: my hair has no particular shape, not in fashion's
terms. I wash it in the stream now and then, and tie it
back with rawhide. It's auburn, sunstreaked. When I hold
out strands I see a lot more grey than I expected. Guess
it's gone pretty grey on top. I'm tall -- five foot eight.
Everything about me is long. Arms, legs, face, nose. My
eyes are hazel. I've let my body hair grow out, dark leg
hair, underarm, hair on my belly. At first it felt odd to let
it grow. I was always stroking it, pulling on it. It made
me feel half animal. Now it is a natural part of me.

Hesitantly I let go of all the image trappings: makeup,
shaving, deodorant. I began to wear the same clothes so
long they became a second skin. I was afraid I would
cease to be. Irrational, I know, but, without a reflection,
how would I know I existed? Without a style, an imprint,
a statement, as the magazines say, how could I *be*?

All alone here, completely vulnerable, I began to have
nightmares about dying. And other things began to come
up with those death fears -- internal reenactments of scenes
which I had long forgotten. Here in my ghost town, for a
period of several months, I was haunted by those

memories. As if by removing myself from a littered existence, I had cleared the way for ancient issues to present themselves and be once and for all dealt with -- although I didn't know exactly how to deal with them, except that, when they came up, I would let them, not fight them.

Like the one about my right breast. My third week here, I woke up one morning to find my right breast was in pain, as if bruised. I wondered if I had perhaps pulled a muscle under my arm, causing the pain, but then a memory suddenly came up, unbidden, before I even sat up in bed. *Oh, so this is what today will be about*, I thought. The memory was of my mother slapping my right breast. I was twelve, the breast was a new, distressing presence for which neither of us had been prepared. My mother had never before hit me, yet there I was with the stinging red print of her hand across my nipple. I stared up in shock at the anger, hatred and regret on her face. Why had she hit me?   And then I fainted, the first of my many such attempts at denial of physical reality during those puberty years.   When I came to, my mother was phoning the hospital, thinking I was dead.

I let my memory recur throughout the rest of the day until I could recall what had prompted her anger. It was because of the way I would flinch if she accidentally brushed against me or reached to straighten my hair. I flinched because I felt she touched me in hatred and repulsion at my budding sexuality. This was not something I could put into words at the time, but something I knew. It was my first lesson in being treated as a sexual being. By men wanting to bed me, or bed whatever image I represented to them. By women who hated me, in sexual competition.   By my mother who saw her waning desirability in my new sexuality. By my father who stopped hugging me when my breasts began.   By

employers who would pigeon-hole me because I was
female. Rarely -- never? -- to be seen as a complete,
whole, human animal, regardless of my sex. This
separation between my body and spirit caused me to view
my sexual needs and desires with anxiety and suspicion.
Wasn't it my body that kept me in separation from the
world of people? The mark of my mother's hand was upon
me, indelibly; I would look down to watch a man sucking
my breasts, awed that I could not *feel* it happening. I
would stand in a mirror, later, and finger my nipples,
watch them harden into points, yet feel no sensation.
These twin beings sprouting from my chest were aliens
with a life apart from me. They drew men toward me,
compelled me through and, by remaining numb, removed
me from, my sexual experiences. I viewed them with
disdain and wished they were smaller.

It wasn't just the condition of being a woman among
humans that drove me away. It was being a human among
humans. Even had I been a man, I believe I would have
left, eventually. We all saw each other as things; we
couldn't seem to get inside of one another. Sometimes on
city buses I would try to examine my fellow passenger as
if he or she was a unique person, a body in formation and
movement, fingerprint, impression, that would exist only
once, never to be repeated. That fat man with slitted eyes
who leered at the prepubescent girls in navy plaid uniforms
-- was he a valuable contribution, a necessary unit to the
whole of life? And the disheveled woman who opened her
shopping bag to dangle a glass necklace before her three-
year-old daughter, then shouted and slapped when the
entranced child reached to touch the sparkly beads -- was
this woman a form without which nothing else would be
possible? Were these humans crucial parts? I wanted to --
needed to -- believe they were. But I could not see it.

The young girls with bruised babies, their mouths as slack as the children's, as if both mother and child continually drank from a narcotic nipple. The men from the halfway house who got on the bus and, before even dropping their token into the slot, began to catalogue the women on this ride, measuring where to take their seat. If my glance happened to fall within three feet of a homeless man's proximity, he took this as an invitation to take the seat next to me. If I disdainfully kept my eyes fixed out the window, he sat in front of me and turned in his seat, his arm thrown over the back, to sullenly stare into my face. Even if I did stick to my resolute silence, the manipulations it took to avoid contact -- (keeping my eyes and jaw tight, not moving my hands in my lap, not shifting in my seat, for any movement, no matter how slight, was considered a sign of interest) -- forced me into a nonverbal dialogue of resistance. It was all my fault, I began to believe, for not being of the moment, for struggling against the culturally agreed-upon "reality." For wanting to preserve my silence and solitude, my privacy and reveries, while being carried in the vinyl chipped seats and scratched metal window frames of the bus, staring through muddied glass at streets I would never walk otherwise. This was my punishment for wanting to escape and deny my harsh environment.

It had reached the point where there was no longer a measure of extreme or slight reaction. My anger was constant, my repression was as everpresent as breathing. Was it the nine-year-old boys hanging on the schoolyard fence who greeted me with mock respect, "Hello, lady," then called out behind my back their sexually violent intentions? Was it the waking in the middle of the night to a man holding a Bic lighter over my face? Was it the nights, eight years later, in which I would sit upright from

a nightmare of a man breaking the windows? Waiting for
my pulse to calm, I would sit in the dark and recall that I
had been having a nightmare on the night of the break-in,
just before waking to the cigarette lighter.

The body knows. Just because the eyes are closed, the
dreams are in control, the limbs lie heavy and sedated,
does not mean what happens in the sleeper's room is not
noted, not reacted to. The dreams take over, encode the
information -- the sliding up of the window; the newness of
night breeze on your skin; the foreign scent; the cat
scuttling under the sofa; the slight jingle of coin as your
purse is opened, the creaking of the floor next to the bed.
These things are noted and the body encodes them into
nightmare. So, eight years later, who is to say it is
paranoia if you wake from a nightmare and sit shivering
and sweating, certain the dream is a warning? Someone is
crouched in the bushes, his feet pressing down the grass
under the window. When your cat looks up toward the
window, startled, it isn't simply a moth or fluttering
cobweb, but another human who has pressed his forehead
against your window, trailing his illness, pain and damage
across the glass like the wet track left by a grey snail on a
rainy night.

It was for these things that I left, and these were the
things that haunted me. To cut through those layers of
how other people perceived me, to unplug the wires of
trigger reaction. I needed to find out if I had ever made a
single choice in my life based on my true, interior, raw,
human life presence.

Sometimes I think I have been healed. Other times I
feel anxieties stirring deeper, and think I have only numbed
myself or avoided it all by letting my role muscles go
slack. If I were suddenly back in their world, I wonder if
I would react the same way again, or if the expectations

would now seem even more extreme, foreign and strange. Would I be immune, or more appalled than before?

All of this came up, distressing, distracting me those first weeks here. I would go to the stream for water and find myself -- minutes? hours? -- later, still crouched by the sunlit water, staring into it, blinded, lost in these wonderings and rehashings at what I had left behind. Tense at being alone, vulnerable. As if those men of the city night streets might follow, come looking for me here. As if there was no safe place on earth. Not even here.

Until I remembered that this was exactly what I had come here for, to be alone. And that being alone meant a kind of safety; I was the only human animal here and I knew what I would do next. If anyone came to visit my ghost town -- (highly unlikely, it is miles from the nearest town, no easy path to it, a difficult mountain pass that keeps it hidden -- I won't say where it is, in case this butcher paper somehow makes it to civilization, except to say it is "somewhere in the southwest") -- anyway, if anyone were to come here, they wouldn't be able to sneak up on me. I would have plenty of warning of their approach. The birds would be still, the quality of the air would change, and I know all the hiding places.

There have been visitors, three times. They seem to show up just at the point when I'm getting low on matches and craving a taste of some food not in my own supply. I don't fantasize about the foods unavailable here, like deli things or shrimp or imported chocolates, but every few months I begin to envision a camper's supply of dried fruit, coffee, salty crackers -- plausible things. And, within a few days, hikers come. (Maybe my hunger is so strong it reaches out premonitory antennae to approaching backpacks.) Once I saw a campfire, about a mile from here to the west. I crept to it and found two men sleeping.

I took an awful chance that they might wake up, but my fingers actually twitched at the thought of what I might find in their backpacks, so I took the risk. They, in turn, slept deeply in exhaustion from their rigorous hike, and in their false sense of security that they were the only humans for several miles. The venture was worth it; I came back to my cabin with chocolate bars, two t-shirts, a bag of beef jerky, a jar of coffee (instant, but better than nothing) and a small bag of pistachio nuts. The chocolate and nuts I stretched out as a weekly treat for two months, a mouthful at a time.

My second visitors I never saw. I heard their voices as they climbed around the old mine shaft -- sounded like three people, a woman and two men. They stayed over-night in one of the cabins at the other end of town. I hid while they were here, nailing boards over my doors on the outside and crawling back in through a window, so it would appear no one was here. Although it was chilly I didn't light my woodstove for two days and only left my cabin -- to raid theirs -- while they were at the mine shaft. No coffee, unfortunately, but packages of mint tea were a different treat, six homemade raisin cookies, a small bag of sugar, cornflakes and powdered milk. I ripped the packages to make it appear an animal had been the culprit, and did not dare take the things in cans or containers only a human hand could open, for fear they might begin a search for me throughout the town. I had hoped for another chance to ransack their backpacks after they were packed to leave, so that they wouldn't notice the missing goods until they were several hours away, but they left before sunrise while I was asleep. That was a frustrating encounter, for they had, among the three of them, supplies I coveted.

My last visitors were young honeymooners from

Wisconsin. I liked their looks, actually, and I was so close
to them I heard what they talked about.   I was upstairs in
the old saloon, crouched under the window, right above
them when they stopped to eat from their backpacks on the
porch. As I breathed softly and adjusted my feet so as not
to crunch the dead flies -- the slightest noise carries here --
I grinned at the irreverent way they talked about the
wedding ceremony their parents had put them through, and
the way they wistfully speculated how it would be to live
here. And whether there were ghosts. They said they
thought that it wouldn't scare them, they respected ghosts.
Even camping, the woman wore nail polish, three large
silver rings, and a lot of eye makeup. She posed, walked
away from her new husband, sulking, sultry, pretending to
be absorbed in fingering a bone shard. Pelvic bone, from
a cow. She felt his eyes on her spine and just barely let
her body sway. Tight rein, just enough to suggest her
hunger. Hands in her pockets, like a cigarette billboard
man. I liked her. She was a lot like I used to be, A
Woman. Only she had been playing it longer than I, had
committed to it. A lot of people would respect me for
walking away from everything, I guess. They would think
it was damned hard to do. Maybe it takes another kind of
courage to play out the role you've chosen, maybe improve
on it. Walking away was easy, I had always wanted to.

I squelched the urge to expose myself to the couple.
All you need is one little rumor that a weird woman is
living in a ghost town and soon the television crews arrive
in helicopters. I kept quiet and they moved on. First they
bathed in my stream on the edge of town. I followed them
there and watched from the old mine company office a few
yards away, where, accomodatingly, they left their
backpacks. He was beautiful in the sunlight.

I thought a lot about sex for several days after they left. I lay by my campfire (lit with their "Western Inn" matches), sipping their coffee and chewing their dried figs, remembering sex in a kind of vague, clinical way. Sex gets dusty in the mind if you go without it for long. Important in another time, another climate. After you've been away from Western society's version of it, it becomes more of a body thing, not so much Madison Avenue. If I were out walking in my woods and came across a naked man bathing in the stream, there would be no time to think first or fantasize, rationalize or decide. We would just go for each other, not a word said before or after. At least that's how I imagine it would be...

...Isolation breeds its fantasies, same as does proximity. Two different kinds of isolation, that's all. Only, I really do think that kind of immediate, unencumbered, physical encounter *is* possible in this ghost town. Not possible in a city. Not that way.

My heart is beating faster, I smell my heat-sweat, at what I've written here. Christ! The slightest introduction of the barely mentioned *idea* of a male in my proximity and this is my condition?

I should be on my knees, apologizing to some male muse that I've made come, on my hands, down my belly, premature. A funny word, "premature." Premature never bothered me, the times I experienced it. In my hands, down my belly, raw, uninhibited, uncontrollable. It delighted me. So rare, to experience those moments of purity, minus technique, minus macho, minus all the sex manuals, minus everything. Just something raw happening, out of control. The man would laugh, embarrassed, or apologize. But I ached for those moments. One of the quirks of my hunger. Hunger for anything that might happen between people without masks or ritual or fear.

Anything. Imperfection, an awkward movement of a torso, a phrase incoherently uttered. Only in those moments did I feel fully alive, responsive. Unrehearsed, real, hurting moments. And I kept it very, very secret, that ache. On the surface, I was cool. Under my makeup and clothes.

The noon sun is blinding me and my fingers are cramping. My handwriting looks familiar, a bit shaky, smaller than I remember it, but that's to compensate for the limitations of the roll of butcher paper. I could use coals from my fireplace if I run out of pencils, and cover the faded newsprint wallpaper walls of this town with my story. Then I could lie down with charcoal in hand at the last wall, the last sentence, "To be continued in saloon." I've been the only one here, no witnesses. The world would never know if my story was truth or fantasy. Whether I was sane or raving.

2. Bones

This evening I'm writing in the "om Bartlebaugh II" bone room, on the second story of the old hotel. (That's what's left of the name on the door, in flaking gilt letters.) Not one of those natural history museum rooms where beetles pick clean the skeletons to later be assembled with identifying cards -- I was in one once, with a lover, back in the world, in Chicago. Horrible smell. Sometimes there is the faint smell of old carcass in here, but nothing as strong as that was. My biologist lover also showed me drawers full of cotton-stuffed hummingbirds in the basement of the Field Museum, lying with their iridescent throats shining colors up at me I hadn't enough crayons in my memory to name. The throat of each was unique, a never-to-be-repeated hue.

He cupped a bird in his palm as tenderly as if it were breathing, and read its name on the tiny white tag. "Oh, this is the same as the last one," he said.

No, I said, this is a color that has never before existed and never will again. Stuffed in a drawer in Chicago. Screaming its choked song to the cedar drawer above it. I wanted to make love to him, right there, in those echoing basement corridors of tiny, silenced, feathered bodies. In the world of men, that was the kind of murder which inspired my hunger.

Bartlebaugh's bone room isn't that sort of bone room. It's a kind of natural history museum, a roadside curio with stuffed owls and rattlesnake skeletons. Even the spiney white balloon of a fugu fish hangs by a wire from a crossbeam. The taxidermied animals on high perches were shredded by moths and other insects long ago. The animals on low shelves were attacked, it seems. Probably a bear or wild cat got in here and thought they were alive. Or some beast in rut, like the old neutered cat I once had who attacked the bathmat, kneaded it like mother's breast, and pushed into it the ghost of his furious seed. Something takes over, doesn't care about the "partner." Dildo, body, bathmat, squirrel skin. The hunger.

I cleaned up Bartlebaugh's museum long ago. Pushed Bartlebaugh's desk so it faces the floor-to-ceiling window which overlooks Main Street. Gathered all the stuffed animals into a huge oak wardrobe against the back wall. Against the side walls are long oak display cases, in which rest large bleached tortoise shells, a few rattlesnake rattles, deer antler and several cow skulls. I left the animal skeletons on the high shelves near the ceiling and hanging from the beams, and let the spiders build from there. Their white threads interconnect the bleached bones, my heaven of fragile white survival lines. This is my chapel. I come here when the sun is at its hottest white. The window frame casts a shadow across the floor, a pattern of white squares. Sometimes I sit on the floor, in the direct center of the pattern, facing the window. It is as close as I come to a religious service.

I thought this would be a good place to write this evening. I can move from building to building and slowly describe my town, instead of using that dull narrative form, where I fit it all into the first couple of paragraphs along with what I look like, what century it is, and some general mood. Like my novels. My life is not what it was when I wrote those books; my writing must not be what it was. "My writing." God, I grew to hate those words. They were my reason, my excuse, my creed, my nemesis. I could not eat, sleep, brush my teeth without defining myself, explaining my presence in this world. I used to tell people that even if I were in prison and had no pencil, no paper, I'd cut a vein and write on the walls with my fingers, even if no one would ever read it. Self indulgent, ludicrous, but perhaps true. For here I am.

But it took me four years to get to this butcher paper. In mankind's world, my writing had become a defensive posture, my protective shield and weapon. My life was lived in distant observation, "taking notes," only fully touched later, at the typewriter or on the yellow pads by lamplight when the world was asleep. Even my emotional reactions to events were often delayed, withheld for the writing process. I came to see that, although writing seemed to intensify my experience by letting me live it twice, it also separated me from my experience. It became important that I find out what it would feel like, what daily existence would be, if I broke the habit of writing. The idea was terrifying, more terrifying than letting go makeup or being utterly alone. Because I had no concept of a life without writing. I would stop breathing, I was certain.

But I began to experience an unexpected joy. The first time I saw a snake, I sat right down to watch it, to really *see* it. I absorbed the details of it, but not to record later. I went through the emotions it aroused -- but not to write them down. I stared at that snake so long, in the high afternoon sun, that it began to shimmer and vibrate. Its markings retreated into the ground around it, perfectly

camouflaged as I watched. The distinction between snake
and soil and even myself, observing, began to fade. I
became so still that the snake forgot my presence and
moved along. And then I moved along, and found myself
smiling. At the beauty of the snake. At the rightness of
the snake to be here in these textures and colors. I had not
come away with a description of a snake for my internal
catalogue, or a scene to fictionalize later, "woman
encounters snake." It wasn't an experience translatable
into another context. It was that particular snake, at that
particular moment, and my particular sensory experience of
it. A private show, just for me. Needing no embellish-
ment, no reconstruction.

So it began to go with everything. The first trout I
caught -- what a moment! I shouted, I laughed, I felt I
might lift off the ground in joy. Then I had to figure out
how to clean it, to calm myself and remember watching my
father do it all those years. All those times I had held the
flashlight on the back porch at midnight while he cleaned
and gutted and told me of the characters he had met on his
trip, I had resonated to the timbre of his voice, mesmerized
by the movement of his fingers and the knife, but I had not
consciously noted the procedure. Now I called upon those
same memories, blocking out his voice and fingers, focused
instead on the steps to cleaning a fish. The first mouthful
of that trout, cooked on my fire that night -- my fingers
twitched to write it down the next morning, to record that
historic moment. But I didn't. I needed to experience the
validity of a life lived once, in the moment, fully present.
I couldn't let myself pick up a pen again until I had
overcome that need to rewrite and find a better word than
the true, original word of experience.

Now I reapproach the same question, but with these
pencils. It is possible that this ghost town will be dis-

covered at a time in history when it will have some importance to the world, something to be reported back. Then
they might find my manuscript, or the writing on the walls.
Each cabin could be a different chapter you could visit and
read as you wished, moving in and out of sequence.
My father brought me photographs of this place when
I was sixteen. He used to fly through this territory in his
Cessna on weekends, mapping out untraveled areas. He
landed in the field east of here, hiked in and took some
black and white photographs. I always kept them. The
front porch of the general store on Main Street, its wooden
floor crosshatched with bands of light from rotted ceiling
planks that had fallen away overhead. From the porch you
could see the spread of Main Street's cabins. Some of the
cabins were intact, others roofless and leaning, still others
collapsed into listless log piles grown over with sagebrush
and bunch grass. Black mine tailing dumps were visible at
a distance, beyond a low wall of dark tumbleweeds blown
up against a barbed wire cemetery fence. Close-up photos
of splintered, glassless window frames set in lime-chinked
log walls. Foundation outlines dotted with chamiso. A
row of brick coke ovens, piles of rusted tin and broken
glass. A lone stone chimney, standing in a circle of
cottonwood trees. My father pointed out that the false
front was all that remained of the old saloon in one photo,
and tapped his forefinger on another photo of a tightly
boarded-up window, laughed and said, "Beyond that
window is a roofless room, a beaten-in rusted wood stove,
and a floor of mesquite." To me these photos were of
another planet, a place I knew I could escape to if -- when?
-- I had had enough of a world in which I felt I was an
alien. That vision stayed with me: the cabin in the woods,
solace, sanctuary. As a child I would whisper the word,
"sanctuary," over and over for the sound of it. All my life

I was moving toward the time when I would have had enough, learned enough, to survive alone in the wilderness. So obsessed was I that, when my father was dying and I went home to be with him, I kept thinking about the map he had drawn of this area. The night he was dying, I went into his study to search for it. He was methodical; it was in a file marked "Ghost Town." Even as he rang for me to come to his bedside that final moment, I was furtively tucking the map into the lingerie pocket of my suitcase.

Somehow his death, six years after my mother's, freed me. I no longer had a parent who required knowledge of my presence and whereabouts in the world. And he had been the only person who knew the ghost town's location. Now I could do exactly what I had always wanted to do, which was to simply leave, escape. Within six months of his death I was here. Some mystery must have surrounded my sudden disappearance, some suspicion of foul play. After all, I had been in a new relationship, working on my third novel, my life was "full and happy" as they say in the suicide articles.

I drove as far in as I could, then made the four-day hike. Of course, it was now over twenty years since my father had been here. The formerly intact cabins were now leaning; most of those which had been leaning in '59 were now log piles; the former log piles were now eroded. The coke ovens had crumbled and the saloon false-front had collapsed. Foundation outlines were almost invisible now, completely choked by chamiso. But there were a few salvagable cabins and the old hotel had essentially withstood nature's assaults. I wasn't dismayed; I had expected these changes. It was, certainly, no longer my father's ghost town. Now it was mine, discovered and claimed by me in this particular stage of its decaying history.

I had no plan, didn't know how long I would stay.

Returning to my jeep twice those first months, I carried
back rations, matches, tools and seeds to start a vegetable
garden. Dad had talked of catching trout here, so I
brought fishing gear. There was a time before my first
harvest when I ran out of rations and survived on fresh fish
and apples from the trees on the edge of town. A wide
variety of food seems necessary in the civilized world;
here, I quickly found that variety had not been a need but
a preference, an old habit born of the same hungers that
fostered constant change -- in clothing, decor, hairstyle. I
had followed the frantic motions of my peers to sample,
claim allegiance to, then quickly discard with a yawn,
certain wines, brands of imported foods, designer labels,
makes of car, neighborhoods. Lovers, even, to match the
current mood. This was all easily put aside when I came
here. Put aside with immense relief. Here, food became
something to cut the ache in my belly -- sustenance, pure
biology, not ritual. I now prefer the cycles of food that I
myself have nurtured, the knowledge that nothing I eat
comes from other hands, other soils, other waters. In this
way I have become integral with the winds, scents and
seasons of my environment. I never tire of the smell of the
fresh garlic I put in the ground, the crisp snap of my
garden's carrots, the apples from trees some miner's wife
planted. And the trout from my stream grow tastier every
year. This has simply become how my world is. Nothing
to exclaim over. And not monotonous.

Except, lately, I have developed a restless longing to
feel another's presence, to see eyes in a face. I remind
myself of all the adjusting and maneuvering required in the
presence of other human animals. Still, I fasten on a pair
of eyes. They don't look into mine; they simply stare off
over my shoulder at something, at nothing, and they allow
me to stare into their nothingness. The way my cat used

to let me, when he stared out a window behind me. Can't
do that with humans. There is always an end to it. They
meet your stare, wrinkle the skin around their eyes, shrug
their shoulders, turn away, laugh. Some inevitable sign of
self-consciousness.

Self-consciousness. The words have a different
meaning for me here than they used to. Not an awareness
of others' awareness of me, which is the most they ever
meant in civilization. Many times I would go walking in
the city to break from my writing, to wrestle through a
troublesome passage. Those were the times I was not
aware of myself, when I was caught in a fiction -- I was
not "a woman" but simply a channel through which words
were moving. I would not put on any makeup for those
walks, would leave my hair twisted up uncombed, throw an
old corduroy jacket over my writing clothes -- comfortable,
baggy pants and sweatshirt. Absorbed in my thoughts, in
no way aware of or projecting myself as a sexual being, to
be suddenly startled and thrown into outrage at the
assaultive sexual noises and obscenities hurled at me from
a passing car. This was self-consciousness. Here in my
ghost town self-conscious means an awareness of my self
beyond an *image* of my self. This is the place (inside, up,
down, out?) I go when I sit in the squares of light here in
the bone room.

Bartlebaugh rented two rooms, according to the
register. A bedroom and a bone room. I wonder if he
charged admission or if the menagerie was only for his
enjoyment. So much about this town is a mystery. Yet so
much revealed. There aren't any clues left in the hotel.
Long ago some enterprising hikers came and took the
collectibles -- tobacco tins, jewelry, bits of tapestry, things
that a backpack could carry. In Bartlebaugh's bedroom I
did find one old book with haunting little drawings, *Old*

Secrets and New Discoveries. It has a chapter on removing bloodstains from cotton, a tortilla recipe, a warning not to share bed with one who is ill (the weakened spirit of the ill sucks the healthy spirit of the well), and a chapter on blood-letting and leeches. A brown-stained book with crisp, chipped pages and a cracked binding, obviously of importance to the taxidermist.

I had trouble sleeping last night. Very strange, as it's been years since I had that problem. Not since living in the city, and that first week adjusting to the night noises here. Back in the city, after the break-in, I kept a lamp on at night. Here there are no street lights, no porch light. Only moonlight. Otherwise, my cabin is dark, within the night's dark. Somehow the totality of the darkness here makes sleep deeper, more imperative. Last night's insomnia is a puzzle. Must have something to do with this writing; am I feeling invaded because my recording, observing self has intruded on the self that wants to exist only in the moment? Perhaps some anxiety also about having opened myself to the potential of ghostly visitors? Not that I worry about my sanity -- in this context, alone as I am and undefined by any particular society, what meaning have those comparative words "sanity" and "insanity"? To whom do I compare my mental state? Bartlebaugh's skeletons? The lizards on the outside wall?

And if I envision for myself a companion, a visitor, if the suggestion of that presence calls up in me -- in my body, my mind, my spirit -- the same responses that a real man would call up, who is to say there is any difference? The imagination in daydreams presents as many frustrations as does reality. A real person compels and attracts. Then, at the very moment something unrehearsed is about to happen between you, he turns his head, appalls you, retreats. In daydreams phantom lovers walk toward you and suddenly your mind is on the grocery list, or the floor caves in, or the conscious mind interferes, editing, "Yes, but a moment ago you were both in an elevator!" The frustration is no different. Only the emotional response is different. With real people you get angry (they didn't fulfill your hunger); with your own fantasy interruptions, you yourself fill that hunger -- change the fantasy channel, switch to hot tub! Man, woman, hot tub, orgasm. No more hunger. It is so easy.

Sometimes. Usually. But not last night. When I had trouble sleeping, I let myself imagine the visitor that might come. I visualized every detail, but his hand kept turning odd colors, first lime green, then purple, then blueblack. I would concentrate on another body part, his ear, his shoulder, but those changed colors also. I could not achieve seriousness, could not hold every part of him before me simultaneously. I let him go and focused instead on the sensations of my fingers on myself. Maybe I will be unable to conjure a ghost, I have become so rooted in my solitude.

I keep thinking I hear voices. Footsteps, a moment ago a woman's laugh at my elbow, very distinct. And the sensation last night, as I orgasmed, that I was being watched, and that sensation making it all the more intense. When I masturbated in my Chicago apartment, I used to pretend that a man was watching. I would arch to his eyes, move in provocation. But I was arching and moving in the ways I had seen in the magazines, in the films. Last night was different from that. Something -- fierce. I lost myself in my movements. They were not of those externalized images of sexuality. Something else happened. I felt I was being watched as I came, but not by a human. Perhaps an animal. A bird, a mouse, a deer outside the window. It is possible, for I seemed an animal, and reacted as to animal eyes.

Could my visitor be an animal? Not the Marlboro man, but a male animal, as I have become a female animal? I keep wanting to open that door, to see him, to let him come in, but it's not the right moment yet. Some other things must be written down before I let him in, before I even begin to build the color of his eyes or how/where in my town I will first encounter him. Of course, first person singular, I will see him first. Although, later he could tell me that he saw me first, that I was unaware. An interesting twist, that he would stalk me, here in my town where I am the one who stalks, who owns, who hides and watches and waits. Anyone who could stalk me on my own territory without my knowing would be a real challenge.

There it is, that talk of stalking. Why do I perceive it as a hunt? That is a throwback to contemporary sexuality -- the hunt, the kill, then boredom. I want to be totally free of all of that, to have something unique, something *new* happen here. Not the ritual, the dance, the pretense. The hunt is all of that. Am I saying I want no preliminaries? To go from aloneness to sudden, unexpected coupling, back to aloneness, and never a word said? Maybe that really is what I mean. How can I ever experience the essence of a sexual union, if I move into and out of it defended and guarded, whether as prey or huntress? How can it ever be pure, with no question that both I and the man are entirely and willingly *present* in that moment of touching and entering? It can't possibly be so, as long as being entered and entering another requires the letting down of our guard -- guard we have justifiably constructed for self preservation. How can we let ourselves be so vulnerable? Yet it seems some vulnerability, something beyond the limits we know between men and women, is necessary for anything different to happen.

I am a transplanted being. I did come here from the world of people; I *am* a product of what I was before.

I remember a session with a marriage counselor once. My first marriage was in trouble, we weren't talking, we had lost interest, were bored with each other. Time for new wine, new labels. But first we tried therapy, like all our friends. One afternoon my husband told the therapist how rigid I was when we went dancing. How for him our dancing together was a ritual, a sexual prelude, and that I would refuse to look into his eyes, making him feel he was dancing alone. I began to think about how I felt, dancing, how I would go off into my own world, avoid anyone's eyes; how I felt I was on display and was uncomfortable unless I removed myself, internally. As I began to talk of this with him and the counselor, I suddenly realized I was describing the same feelings I had when strange men whistled or shouted at me on the street. Going into my internal, private world, pretending to be invisible, but all the while with images of a gun in my hand, or of an invisible shield I would pull up around me as I walked past. The counselor told me to finish the sentence, "When my husband wants me to look in his eyes, I resist doing so because..." I stumbled through the sentence, struggling for each word, not clear about my feelings. But the words moved upwards, out of my mouth with an impetus of their own, until I had laid out on the coffee table between my husband, the counselor and myself, these words: "When my husband wants me to look in his eyes I resist because...I am afraid to be vulnerable...because I expect him to hurt me...because he is a man."

"But I never think of my husband as 'men'!" I cried out. The counselor smiled softly and reminded me, "But he *is* a man." I stared across the room in shock, into my husband's face, expecting him to look dismayed, hurt, concerned at my revelation. His face at that moment called to mind those games in which photos of faces are cut in half, eyes mismatched with lips and jaws, puzzles to figure out which eyes go with which mouths. If I only looked into his eyes at that moment, he was communicating a kind of sympathy. If I looked at his mouth, it was twisted into an ironic smile. He was triumphant! I had just admitted his power, and my fear, and he was glad of it. It affirmed his manhood.

How many years will it take me to slough *all* that off? That memory, that kneejerk reaction to men? Even here, where there are no men, it's a skin I must keep shedding. Every year I twist out of a skin which is closer to perfection, less pock-marked with that other world's illness and cankers.

My guest must be as close to these questions and needs as I, or closer. He must not be fresh from society. Not some neophyte I must train, someone to be alarmed, wooed, comforted. A mountain man, a ghost in a ghost town, an animal man already there, with an even more refined sense of smell than mine.

Someone with new recipes for trout.

3. The Tea Maker

I have seen him. Oh god, this was not how I expected it to be. I had so much more I wanted to write here before he entered. And he is not -- somehow he is not my fantasy. I haven't had time to conjure him, to work on the details. I wasn't sure if I wanted him to be stocky and blond or gaunt and dark -- I wanted to create him. *Damn, I wanted to invent him myself!* And here he is.

As for stalking, how ludicrous! Not turning a corner to find him, loincloth, poised to pounce. Instead I find him standing in t-shirt and jeans making a pot of tea at the Ranford cabin wood stove!

The Ranford cabin is at the other end of Main Street, with the Ranford name carved on a panel of the front door. I went there this afternoon because I remembered seeing a piece of screen on the back porch which I needed to patch a window. I knelt to pry the screen from between two boards and, as I stood, something dark blue, almost invisible in the deep grey interior of the cabin, moved slowly inside the kitchen. I stepped to the door quietly, peered in, and saw him. Or his back, at least, bending to pour boiling tea water into a pot.

The strange part is I somehow knew, immediately, that

this was no ordinary hiker with a backpack for me to scavenge. There have been no signs of his arrival or presence, and he is suddenly here. But, more than that, he pulled my attention in a different way than the hikers did -- something similar to those times back in the real world when I would walk into a room full of people and sense one particular person's presence, in peripheral view, before really looking at them -- a recognition at subterranean levels. This was similar, except the context was not a room full of people but the silence and stillness of my ghost town. He drew my attention so fully that I forgot to be afraid he'd see me, and it is this that has me so disturbed.

Not only does this visitor puzzle me, but the details are odd -- like the look of the teapot. Not a camper's tin, but cream colored, with tiny red flowers clustered on the front, and a chip in the handle. And what about the wood stove fueled up and burning? I didn't see chimney smoke when I walked toward the cabin, nor smell it when I was on the back step. Yet there he was, bending to pour steaming tea.

He didn't seem to see or hear me, which is peculiar. It's so silent here, the slightest noise is heavy on your eardrums, and we were standing only about six feet apart. He should have at least sensed a change in the airflow from the doorway or felt my shadow cross his light. But he didn't turn, just continued his task. I heard the sound of water pouring, saw the steam rising. I pulled back quickly, off the porch, around the cabin, ran back here, and bolted the door. Not the brave, stalking landlady.

After bolting the door, I sat staring at it, as if it might explode inward. Then I laughed out loud, unbolted it, touched my knife in my back pocket, and strode back to the Ranford cabin with my walking stick. To confront my guest, be he real or fantasy.

He was gone. No fire, no steam, no tea. Everything in that cabin kitchen cold and dusty as ever, no sign of anyone having been there in at least sixty years. Except for one thing -- I found the cream colored teapot with red flowers in the back corner of the cabinet. Cold, dry. But real. I suppose I might have seen it there before, on one of my hunts through the town. That might prove it was my fantasy; my subconscious could have included that detail.

I haven't even seen his face yet. From the back, he was quite tall, long-waisted, his long arms tanned, hands wide with prominent veins, from work that built up the finest muscles and tendons. The hair along his forearms dark. Blue t-shirt, faded denims, brown hiking boots. His hair was similar to mine, auburn and grey, pulled back with a rubberband in a ponytail. I glimpsed a beard from the side. I recall his scent, very strong but pleasant, the scent of slept-in, sun-warmed, unwashed cotton. I wonder if mine is similar. I soak my clothes once a month or so in the stream; a familiar body scent always lingers in them, diluted.

This is so unnerving, but much more interesting than my arranging everything. What feeling did I get from him, making tea, silent? He wasn't thinking, exactly. He seemed completely involved in the tea-making, lost in it. If he was real, why then didn't he acknowledge me? Or have *I* become a ghost after all this time?

That clean teapot. Not a fingerprint, not a gritty spot of dust on it...

Late afternoon rain. My favorite time. Sometimes it stops me completely, the rain. I go to my bed and wrap in my sleeping bag to keep off the chills of excitement. Even now, they come, after four years. I sit huddled against the wall, listening to the tin dance on the roof, exhilarated, a child again. "Sanctuary!" I have escaped!

Just now a dark cloud passed over the sun and a breeze came up, increasingly cool. The trees are beginning to sway, an ocean sound if I close my eyes. There's that rain smell. Someone once told me the smell of rain is an organism that opens up in moist air and gives off its perfume. I always thought it was a wet asphalt smell, yet here it is, in the middle of my Walden.

There! Thunder over behind the mountain!

When the storm began this afternoon, I stopped writing, poured juniper tea (from a bush near Ranford's cabin) and sat on my back porch to watch it. The porch faces the woods, and the stream runs behind them. It is so quiet here I can hear the water at night.

I was staring toward the woods, mesmerized, not really thinking of anything. Something moved in the trees, a vague, light-colored shape. I tried to focus on it, but it pulled back and I only saw the blurred outline of pine trees in the rain. Watching the storm was all I wanted to be doing, none of that encounter defensiveness, no worrying about my tea-maker. I shook the anxiety off my shoulders and made myself look in another direction. There it was again, on the periphery. It seemed to stay now, so I slowly turned my head. He was there. Standing naked on the edge of the woods, staring out into the rain. My heart did a double beat and my mouth went dry. Although he seemed to stare straight at me, he made no sign that he saw me. Something in his hands, a piece of clothing, held so that I could only partially see the dark hair below his belly. It was the tea-maker, no question. Same height, arms, beard. Just a white blur against the grey, but definitely he. Solid, water and trees moving behind him, against him, he the only thing not moving. I stared until I was convinced that our eyes locked. He still didn't move. Finally, after several minutes, I decided to stand up, to *make* him acknowledge that he saw me. Before I could move to do so, he turned his head, looked to the side, to the ground. He moved his shoulders as if they had an ache, shook out the wet shirt in his hands, and pulled it on, a long-sleeved white shirt. He turned and walked back into the woods, buttoning it as he went, nonchalant. If he'd seen me he didn't care. I stood, quickly, hoping he might turn back. I couldn't believe this was to be all of our encounter. I stood for a very long time, staring into the woods as the rain receded.

I pulled on my mud boots, got my walking stick and knife and walked to where I had seen him. I continued back into the woods, the way I'd seen him go, looking to the ground for signs, listening. If there had been footprints, the mud showed nothing now. I walked to the stream. Still nothing.

It has unnerved me a little. These things as they occur seem real, while they're in motion, without question. Afterward, I look back and realize there is something surreal, doubtful. If I hadn't been acting on the emotion of the moment -- (looking for food or trying to avoid being eaten) -- I would have realized the unreality of it as it occurred, might have seen it as a waking dream, a hallucination. It's too coincidental that, within twenty-four hours of beginning this journal and calling upon ghostly visitors, suddenly should appear a man. There's been no one here in over a year, not since that couple. I don't know if I invented this man; I don't know if he is real.

When I first came to my ghost town, I was open to this sort of thing, to not knowing what would happen next. I *wanted* the unknown to happen. Then after a while I got used to being in control, being landlady and mayor of my town, knowing what would happen each day. I don't like having this stranger here, not knowing where he'll turn up next, what planet he's from, whether he means harm or good.

Mostly, I don't like not knowing whether he'll be gone when I wake up tomorrow.

And I don't like caring whether he'll be gone.

I've got to get control here. There's only one thing to do. I have to comb this town from one end to the other, every cabin, room, shed, and find him. Find out exactly what he's doing here. I won't just sit here in my cabin waiting and wondering.

In front of me here on my writing table, next to my Coleman lantern, is a six-inch tall wooden carving of me. My face, my hair, my long arms and legs, my clothes. Details that terrify me, the kinds of details you only catch if you see me up close. Painted, even. Grey in my hair, the green patch on my jeans knee, the red shoe laces on my hiking boots.

I went through every cabin before sunset, moving quickly. Every room in the hotel, every shed, the one barn that's standing, the old chapel. Didn't have time to go through the woods, the sun was setting fast. The last cabin I checked was Ranford's, where I saw the tea-maker yesterday. Nothing looked any different there. I started to leave, then felt pulled back to look at that teapot again. Not sure what I expected, just felt compelled.

One thing I've learned to do here in my town is to act on my gut feelings. Too many times in the city I regretted not doing so. So much there kept me from it, as if the noises of the city and my own restless thoughts blocked me from hearing my inner voice. Out here there have been times when it has literally saved my life. I sense when a

snake is near. More than once I've stood still with that
feeling and have seen a rattler glide past, just inches away.
I've found a lot of useful things in my town by following
my voice when it tells me to open a certain drawer or
closet door, or look under a pile of rubble. Sometimes
when I don't have the right tools or supplies to fix
something, I go on a hunt in my town and my voice leads
me to the strangest objects. After thinking a minute or
two, I realize they are exactly what I need to finish the job.

I listened to my voice, walked over and opened the
cabinet. Next to the teapot stood the doll. I jumped back
with my hand on my mouth, stifling a scream, then just
stood there, staring at it. I stayed there a long time, until
it was almost dark, staring at the doll until everything else
in the room blurred and went white at the edges. The
small figure seemed to glow in the dusk.

I started to walk out of the cabin and leave it there.
Of course, the tea-maker had made it and he'd be back to
see if I took it. If I did, that would signal a communication between us, and would mean I accepted his
presence. Since I didn't even know who this man was or
how he came here, I wasn't sure I wanted to make that
connection. And if I'd made this man up, but this doll
turned out to be real -- if I reached out my hand and my
fingers closed around a solid object -- then what the hell
did that *mean?* Or if the man was real, then the doll meant
he'd seen me and wanted to connect with me, and what did
that mean? He could be anything, a rapist, a murderer.
Even a biologist.

Of course, I had to take the doll. For one thing,
having stared at it so long in the setting sun, its silhouette
remained on my retina and I could hardly see to walk.
And I was too damned curious. Flattered, too, I guess. I
mean, it was the first externalization I'd seen of myself

since I'd broken all the glass. I was curious to see what I
looked like to a stranger, even if I'd invented him!   I
stuffed the doll in my denim jacket and, in case its creator
was watching, walked nonchalantly back to my cabin. He
didn't have to know right off whether I'd taken it or not.
So here the doll and I sit, staring at each other. The
more I look at it, the more I don't think it's much of a
likeness. I thought it was before, thought the details were
really good. Well, some of them are, but it doesn't really
capture me the way it would if someone who really knew
me carved it. It's a fantasy of what a ghost town resident
would look like, the face both distrustful and curious. The
breasts are larger than mine. Christ, he's even carved on
little nipples under her shirt!   I don't know, this thing
could really disturb me. I wonder when he saw me. Was
it when I caught him making tea or was it during the
storm, from the woods?
Wait a minute! The shoes -- these little red shoe laces
-- I was wearing those *last week*. This week I'm wearing
brown laces. The red ones broke too many times and the
knots made them too short, so I put the brown ones in.
That means he carved this from seeing me *last* week! And
I only first saw him *yesterday*!   This can't be!   It's
impossible that someone could live here a whole week
without my knowing...
...what day was it that I changed shoe laces?
Last...well, who knows what day it was, but it had to be
at least a week ago. And this week I've been wearing my
mud boots, not my hiking shoes, with all this rain.
This also means he arrived here before I began this
journal. Did I compel him, or did he compel the writing?

Damn. Now I really am disturbed. Where the hell *is*
this guy? Not a sign of anyone living in any of the cabins.

Must be staying in the woods. But he was making tea in the Ranford cabin. What about that? I checked that kitchen afterwards and there wasn't a single fingerprint in all that dust on the counter and table and wood stove. The coals in that stove were old and cold, I checked them. It is strange that the teapot should have been covered with dust from sitting all those years in the cabinet, but it was wiped clean. Unless he brought it with him, but backpackers don't carry heavy china teapots.

This is damned strange. Am I finally losing it? Cabin fever, mirages? Alone so long you start to get funny?

What am I getting scared for? Isn't this what I've always wanted, always suspected? That the borders of "reality" and "fantasy" are all in our heads? That the only way to experience anything of value is to somehow cross those borders?

He must be staying in the Ranford cabin, and was hiking or hiding out when I went there.

I don't like the way this is going at all. I wanted to focus on the *writing* of this. I wanted to make up this man, this visitor, and have this thing happen between us. I didn't make an outline. That was the whole point, *not* to plan it out in advance, to go from one word to the next and see what happened. Now here is this external force, this *intruder*, who, by simply walking into my town, has changed the whole course of my existence, which I have taken such pains to keep in my control. I should ignore his presence, or ask him to leave, and get on with what I started, my *own* man, my *own* vision, my *own* working out of whatever I'm working out by being here in the first place. Instead, just as I did in the real world, I'm dancing the old dance, the old hunt, the old adapting, maneuvering, second-guessing. Is this what I'm to learn here? That I haven't changed a goddamned bit? That I'm still a "civilized" woman? Am I going to start picking through the charcoal to make mascara and bruise my lips with wild berries?

I don't like this doll. She's ugly...no, not ugly. Striking, I guess. The eyes are dark and alarming. At least not alarmed, at least not some simpering gothic flower. Alarm*ing*, a female animal with whom to contend. I wasn't expecting to see that in my face. But then, I really don't know what I look like. It's been three years since I looked at myself. I never thought photos of myself, back there, looked like me either. Guess this is the same thing. Is it something innately human, that we can't see ourselves? Not something of Madison Avenue, but something innate? I want to do that, to separate out what is innate and what is induced. To accept -- to choose -- the innate and be able to reject the induced.

Maybe this *is* a good time for a mirror...him, I mean, this guest, this carving. Maybe I can find out what I've become since I came here to my ghost town.

If I could just be certain whether he's real or imagined -- but, wait! I just realized. Whether he's flesh and blood or fantasy, *he is here because I brought him here.* I was ready for a human encounter. That restlessness, that insomnia, those recent dreams from which I awoke gyrating my hips. I was ready, even if I didn't want to admit it, for an encounter. So he came. And if he got here a few days before my consciousness focused on my hunger, well, moving space and time around is part of overcoming those boundaries I want to overcome.

Maybe he thinks he came for his own reasons. Some guy curious about the ghost town, a hiker, a traveler, someone, like me, who wants to live alone. If that's his idea, he'll have to leave, go find his own. This is *my* town. Anyway, whatever he thinks his reasons are for

being here, he's really here *for me*. To tell me something,
to answer whatever my question is about...

...What *is* it about? Men and women? I always
thought so, back there. That I was in pursuit of some
answers and some fulfillments about me and a man. I
certainly put enough time and energy into that.

I'm not sure anymore it's just about men and women.
Or love. Or sex. It's something that's supposed to happen
beyond sex and love. Something else. Something more.
I don't know what it is, but I have always yearned for it,
and sometimes thought I'd found it. Thought a communion
was happening between me and a man. I'd try to talk
about it. He'd deny it, look scared. We'd argue, we'd
impasse, he'd leave.

It's something about human to human. Or human to
animal. Animal to animal? Some nonverbal sharing or
joining. Facing each *other* but looking, not *into* each
other's eyes, but *through* each other's eyes, into something
larger. Back there it seemed we always got stuck at the
into...stuck on the clothes, the image, the trappings, the
body, the s-e-x-u-a-l-i-t-y...and then nothing. Silence.
Familiarity. Maybe comfort, maybe boredom...but nothing
happening.

I still don't know what it is or if it can happen in this
world. This doll stares at me as I write. She's hard and
stiff, in a fixed position. A defensive position, her arms
out slightly, her legs spread apart. Like she's blocking an
entrance.

4. Fire

The inside of my cabin was different when I woke up this morning. I could feel it before I got out of bed.

Of the twenty cabins still standing, in various stages of decay, this one appealed to me most. One side faces the woods, the other side leans in -- literally; the walls are warped at a comical angle -- toward the center of town. I live on the line between my own skeletal "civilization," and the wilderness, the animal realm. There's something I like about the feeling of "going into town" when I take my walks. Since this is the side of town I first entered through, to me, it is the entrance. And my cabin is in the guardian position.

When I moved in here, I washed down the walls and floors with stream water boiled on the wood stove. I scrubbed the outside of the stove, made a broom with reeds tied to a stick, gathered feathers for a duster, and swept out the dirt. There was some furniture -- a metal bed, part of a mattress I stuffed with dry leaves and sewed up. My sleeping bag to sleep on top of when it's hot, inside of when it's cool. I had some cooking things in my backpack and scavenged more from the other cabins. My cabin came equipped with a cast iron kettle. It is a good feeling to use something that is a part of the cabin's history. Bit by bit I've added touches. Wove window shades from stream-edge cane, made a patchwork rug from Bartlebaugh's bear skins. In the spring there are wildflowers on the table, in the winter an arrangement of red rocks and dried branches.

This morning I got up and walked through my cabin -- the bedroom, the big room with the woodstove and corner kitchen -- slowly, touching the walls, seeing it as if I were a stranger. Cozy, despite the roughness, what the sophisticated world calls "rustic." Of course I have to push an occasional reptile out the door with my walking stick, and rain buckets are permanent fixtures.

I'm not sure why I felt uneasy in my cabin this morning. Did I think maybe he'd come here in the night? Or was I imagining how he'd see it if he does come here? What the hell will we say to each other? Nothing, I hope. At least I want to have that much of my earlier fantasy, to have a wordless encounter. Words would lead to questions. We would exchange names and histories. Then we would start talking of other places, people and events, distracting ourselves from the moment-by-moment encounter of each other *here,* now. Words would be easy to misinterpret, not like the pure language of eyes and touching. No, I want no words with him.

It was dawn when I awoke. The light always wakens me, and the birds. The robins in the trees near the window start it up, those in the field join in, and finally all the birds in the woods across the field. I began my day as usual, listening, smiling. My morning music. Then my eyes shot open when I remembered the doll from the night before and realized that I was no longer alone. Someone else in this town was probably waking up at the same moment, listening to the same music, thinking about coffee, as I was.

Or tea.

At first I felt angry. After all I had gone through to
adjust to being the only human here, to now adjust to
another's presence? (Emotion? Instinctive, territorial
protection of my hunting grounds.) Then I felt fear, as I
sat up, remembering that he'd been here at least a week,
and I hadn't known it. (Instinct of prey.) Finally, as I
came fully awake, a thrill of excitement, wondering what
would happen today. (Psychosexual salivary glands.)

I had taken the doll, and now the connection was
made. Whose turn was it? He made the doll and left it.
I took it. I laughed outloud at the complexities of two
humans trying to create a new language: it was either my
turn to respond to the doll, or his turn to respond to my
taking it. Respond to the doll? How? I'm no good at
wood carving, not even any good at drawing. Was I to
write him a note? What would it say? "Come for tea, 2
p.m., last cabin to the east?" Ridiculous. Anyway, I
didn't want to use words to respond. That would lead to
talking, and I didn't want to talk.

I pondered it as I built the woodstove fire to boil
coffee water and warm up biscuits. I stepped outside to
see if there had been any changes in my town during the
night. Some new tumbleweeds pushed against my front
door. Must have been a big wind while I slept. Nothing
else, no footprints but my own.

I drank three cups of strong coffee. Usually I only
allow myself a half a cup and run the water through again
for a weak second cup, or switch to herb tea, to ration the
precious dark grounds. This morning my preoccupation
threw me back into old habits. Chewing on a biscuit, I
stood on the back porch, staring out into the woods.
Nothing came to me. I rolled up a piece of butcher paper,

stuck a couple of pencils in my pocket, and headed for
Bartlebaugh's. Maybe writing about it would help me
think of something.

When I first explored the hotel four years ago, I
discovered a large brass key ring on a peg under the lobby
desk, way back in a corner where the scavengers hadn't
found it. The funny thing was, when I'd gone upstairs
with the keys, the only room in the hotel that was locked
was Bartlebaugh's bone room. It seemed odd that the
thieves who had come here through the years hadn't beaten
the door down to find its treasures. Of course, animals had
gotten in, through the second story window. But I was the
first human to set foot in the museum in -- how many
years? It's one of the reasons it became my chapel. A
truly sacred place. I keep the key on a chain around my
neck. Even though I'm the only human here -- or was,
until the doll maker's arrival -- it's important to me to
know I have the only access to the bone room. Just the
spiders and me. The window is closed now -- opened
while I'm there, but closed each time I leave. One of the
few remaining glass windows.

When I came to Bartlebaugh's today the door pushed
open without my turning the key. A chill rushed through
my body. My sanctuary, the humanless place trespassed
upon. Maybe he was still inside. I stepped through the
door cautiously and stared around the room for signs of
intrusion. I opened the wardrobe and kicked at the pile of
skins. No fingerprints -- this is one place, besides my own
cabin, that I keep dusted. He had definitely been here, I
could feel it. How had he gotten in? I examined the lock.
No signs of a break-in, although he could have picked it.
Anything is possible. Or, assuming this was all part of my
visionary guest adventure, reality might have been

suspended long enough to allow him to simply walk in, through the locked door, or to dissolve its locked condition.

I sat down to collect my thoughts. The challenge was to stop trying to answer all these reality-based questions. It didn't matter how he came to my town or how he got into the bone room. I wasn't even sure if it mattered that he *had*. It was still my chapel. I sat at the table facing the window. And then I saw it, on the window ledge, leaning into the corner. A six-inch-tall image of the doll maker, partner to my doll. I picked it up and laid it on the table. He was very good at catching his own likeness. Of course, I'd only seen him from the back, clothed, and then naked at a distance. But this was him, as I'd seen him, the way he held his shoulders, the way his hair pulled into a ponytail, his legs slightly bowed. I stared at the face; if the artist was true, I'd now see the face which I hadn't yet seen.

A good face. Something familiar about it. Lean cheekbones, full lower lip, a bit of a laugh, long nose, heavy brows. Grey in his hair, like mine. Full beard, reddish. Hazel eyes. Like mine.

So this was the response to my taking the doll. The next step in the dance. Giving me himself, his vision of himself. I wasn't sure what we were communicating. Except it didn't feel threatening. A man who left carved dolls lying around didn't seem up to no good. Not up to anything predictable, either, but he might have a sense of humor, at least.

It bothered me, the idea of his having been in my sanctuary. It felt as bad as if he'd been in my cabin. I froze at that thought. It was quite possible that he *had* been in my cabin. If he'd been here a week without my knowing it, he could have been anywhere he wanted, and

there were plenty of hours I was away from my rooms.
He might even have read the pages of butcher paper!
Quickly I tried to remember if there had been any signs
they had been touched. This was the third day of working
on them. The first day, I'd left them lying open in my
cabin. The second day I'd carried them to and from this
room. Right now they were under my mattress. Stupid,
stupid! The first place anyone would look. Of course, if
he was a good person, meant no harm, why would he look
under my mattress? Still, there was no question: I must
go home immediately and hide those pages.

There's a loose floorboard in the back of the closet in
my cabin. I had a feeling to look there when I moved in,
and found a muslin sachet filled with wild rose petals, three
pearl buttons, and a tiny silver cross. I'd put them back,
felt they might be some magical cornerstone that held the
cabin together. That was where I could hide the pages.
The worst thing that could happen at this point was for this
man to read what I'd written. I laughed as I thought this.
Here I was, looking for a real connection, something
beyond the sexual games and rituals of the real world, and
my first thought was to hide the truth from him. To play
a game. To pretend surprise at his presence? To deny that
I had brought him here? And then what?

That was the question: and then what? Where was
this leading, this intrusion that I accepted, indeed, had
invited? Was it going to be that purely physical encounter
in the woods? And, if so, what was the quality of that to
be? Rough? Forced? The Safeway gothic paperback
wilting, then opening? Weren't we already, immediately,
engaged in a chase? Were the dolls no more than flowers
and candy? How many dolls would it take before I "gave
in," "trusted"?

"Trust." Interesting word. Something one does -- to?

about? because of? -- someone else. Trust that what? That he wouldn't hurt me, physically, emotionally? (Would he fill my hunger? Refuse to? Overfeed it? Or feed it the wrong food?) What would be "to hurt" in this situation, in this ghost town? We couldn't exactly have right or wrong intentions. Or could we? At this very moment, in fact, I could "lead him on" or "push him away." In fact, my every action from this point forward was open to severe scrutiny and interpretation. Already I had started something in motion, by taking the first doll. I had accepted the flowers. Now the candy.

But, damn, this dance was exactly what I'd wanted to *avoid*! I wanted something straightforward -- but without words -- to happen. This was anything but straightforward, although it was, so far, wordless. (Except for these pages.) Subtle, secretive, tantalizing, teasing. Every movement open to *mis*interpretation. I realized I should have left the doll with the teapot. I should have turned away when I saw him naked -- for it now seemed clear that he *had* seen me watching him that day in the rain. That day? Yesterday, only yesterday. He was staring at me as much as I was staring at him. Because he'd already seen me, already knew about me, probably at that moment had already carved the doll. The paint was dry when I found it, only a couple of hours later.

Still, all this mystery of his origins, his nature. How did he make tea or the illusion of tea without starting up the Ranford wood stove, without leaving fingerprints or traces of water? How did he walk into the bone room without a key?

These dolls were painted. The full implication of that suddenly hit me, that this desert hiker carried modern acrylic paints. Of course, the quality of the dolls: a crudeness to them, but an expert crudeness, a practiced carving hand. Somehow that eased my fears. The man was an artist. A maker of tea and a maker of dolls. What was there to fear from that?

But I hadn't been away from men *that* long. I remembered the treachery of which such gentle hands were capable. The strangling of hummingbirds, the ear turned away, the sudden cold mask...

Which was why I didn't want to talk with this man. No words. Not a single word. And, since he was part of my vision, since I had something to do with bringing him here, it would just have to be so. He would have to know not to talk. Whatever was to happen between us, *no words*.

Well, I did take the doll maker's self-portrait back to my cabin. Stuffed into my jacket pocket again, but this time I didn't walk so nonchalantly. I didn't look around, didn't let on I was watching for him, but walked slowly, contemplatively. Until I realized what I was trying to convey to his hidden eyes and got angry with myself and with him. That damned external image consciousness again. Where did body image and body language separate? Or did they? Could that be an innate thing? That posing, that non-verbal dance. I hoped to god not. But perhaps it was.

I strode angrily, quickly, home.

The dolls are standing, side by side, on the bedroom window ledge. Not in here, in open view, so I don't have to keep looking at them and thinking about him. Every hour I let myself walk in there and look at them, at how they change in the varying degrees of light as the sun moves across the sky, or the sky moves across the sun, whichever it is. The paints are happy colors, childhood colors, and they glow in the sunset.

More of a balmy night than a really cool one. Good night for a fire out back. Sometimes in such weather I broil my trout and toast biscuits on a sharpened branch over the campfire. A few yards from the cabin I uncover my fire pit and fill it with tumbleweeds for kindling. I bring the matches, light the weeds, and slide in a log, a half bottle of tequila by my side.

Salt and limes would be nice. In a couple of weeks I'll have to gear up for my semi-annual supply hike into the little settlement west of here. It takes me over a week, and I time it to arrive at sunset. I rest a couple hours in the small wooded area at the outskirts, then begin my evening raid. The settlement is a few miles from a fishing area, yet not actually within it. It consists of nothing more than one cabin, one ranch and a defunct-but-inhabited farmhouse, each several miles apart. Actually, I can't even call it a settlement -- there are no telephone lines, no post office. No signs of any initiative to create a civilized touchpoint, other than a tiny shack near the highway with a gas pump and a limited inventory of groceries, fishing tackle and hardware items. The locals are somewhat reclusive themselves -- although the owner of the gas and grocery operation apparently lives in the cabin a few yards beyond; I have never seen him -- or any other human being -- during my raids on the little store.

I fill my backpack with enough salt, flour, lard, twine, tackle, socks, coffee, tequila and chocolate bars to get me through the next six stringently-rationed months. I leave money on the counter, so it isn't really stealing, and to keep from having to explain myself to the locals -- although I suspect they would understand, and would just as well not deal with me either. I was afraid they would start barring the windows or install a guard dog after my first couple of visits, but it is such a small place, a kind of trusting place, and since I do leave the money, apparently they don't mind. I've actually always felt a kind of magic about it, that it's there for me, only for the labor of the several days' hike. Hiking back takes longer, with a full pack. I go slowly and with no anxiety; I have befriended time.

I sit cross-legged and stare into the fire, lost in its crackle and heat. In a while I'll bring out something to cook. Not really hungry yet. Not for food, anyway. I want the blur of tequila tonight. This being some kind of occasion, an occasion of bewilderment, of things on and in the air unresolved. Anticipation tingles through my spine and pelvis, for, surely, the man will come soon, and something will happen. I've resigned myself to that. I've suspended my irritation at the gestures of civilized courtship. *I* am the one who's cast that off, not necessarily he. What else does he know but those gestures? How else can he approach a strange woman living alone in a ghost town? To him I must be a kind of wild animal, a new species, no predicting how I will react to his movements. He's not stupid; he has chosen quiet, careful ways to tame.

I think of it as that. Today I remembered Saint-Exupery's *The Little Prince*, the part about the taming of the fox. Except the doll maker has not followed the prime lesson of the fox: he has not appeared at the same place every day at the same time. He does leave me with some apprehension in that I never know when or where he will turn up.

I'm not sure what happened. I must have dozed off. The warmth of the fire, the tequila … then I felt something, a change in the air, heat from another source. I opened my eyes and saw I was lying curled up in a circle of orange light. Silhouettes of weeds and bushes circled

the edge of light from the outer darkness. There, at the
edge of the circle, only feet away from me, on the other
side of the fire, stood the man. He stood still and soft and
naked.

At first I could not see his eyes in the shadows of his
heavy brow, but then they caught the firelight and gleamed
out at me, shining. His lips almost smiled, partly sure of
welcome, an animal pulled from the woods by the firelight,
but cautious not to intrude. When he saw I was awake, he
didn't move away or step closer, but stood at the edge of
the light. I stared into his eyes and then, very faintly, so
faintly I wasn't certain it really happened, he lifted his
chin, his smile wavered, exposing the white of his teeth --
longish teeth, the kind that might have been braced in his
youth -- in a way that touched me in the pit of my
stomach. Something broke inside of me, fragile china, and
its contents spilled into me, thick, warm and flooding. The
gesture of his chin, so quick and soft, had said, "Go ahead.
Look."

I did look. It was surreal. That a man would be
standing at the edge of my desert fire, naked and soft.
That I would not be afraid, that he would not be -- hard.
He was not hard. He was not challenging. He was not
there to *do* or *hurt* or *get*. Somehow that was so clear,
while the edges of his body were so vague in the firelight.
I let myself look at him, openly, as if examining a new
animal that had stepped out of the woods. With that same
scrutiny. To find out what it was made of, to fill in all
those telling details before it found its fear and darted back
into the trees.

His shoulders were solid, his chest a bit fleshy and his
nipples soft. Nothing hard here, nothing erect. I followed
the line of his body hair -- in the firelight it was light-
colored, but in sunlight it would be the same dark auburn

as the hair on his head -- from his neck down to his belly.
Between the pelvic bones his hair expanded into a circle,
a full eclipsed moon, and, at the horizon of it, his penis.
Uncircumcised, soft, hanging askew, his balls heavy
between his legs which stood apart. Solid legs, dark, thick
hair, like my own. His calves were round and heavily
veined. His feet disappeared into the night grass.

And then he was gone. Before I looked back up to his
face, to read his reaction to my travels down his body, he
stepped back into the dark beyond the circle and was gone.
I rose quickly, rushed around the fire to where he had
stood. A scent on the air from his body, a strong male cat
scent. But he was gone and I couldn't hear a sound but the
crickets and frogs in the stream.

I turned, stared into the dying fire. Had this been
real? I began to feel I was coming out of sleep. That I
had dreamed the whole thing and even stood and walked in
my sleep. Yet the details, the body, had been so specific
a body, not a body I had ever known before...he must have
been real.

I came in to write this down.

As it was happening I wasn't aware of my physical
reaction. When I stood to follow him, warmth gushed
instantly cool down my inner thigh. I touched my leg and
smelled my fingers. The distinct scent of the hunt, a scent
I have not known in a very long time. For so long I have
not touched myself -- that one night, last week, the first
time in almost a year. And I felt an animal watching me
that night. I am certain now it was he. At my window.
He has watched me several times, sleeping. Everything is
beyond my control now.

I have seen him.

5. Water

Another strange dream tonight. I call them dreams; they are so surreal, other worldly, unexpected, that, afterward, they don't seem possible. Even the quality of remembering them is not the same quality as memories of real events.

Today I bathed in the stream and rinsed my clothes. I washed my hair, using the mint soap I carefully hoard. The heat of the afternoon left a minty sweat on my skin. My shirt carries that deep smell from my body that never completely washes out. I like it. I have *grown* to like it. A familiar thing, a proof of my existence.

Tonight I built a fire again. I took off my clothes and sat, buddha style with the last of the tequila. Then I thought, if he is to see me, I should be reclining. I started to move into a seductive position, then stopped myself. There it was again, that Hollywood crap. How seductive could a woman look, with her body hair all grown out, no white lace hose or garter belt? I remained as I was, swilling tequila and staring into the fire.

I sat there a very long time, beginning to feel ridiculous because he wasn't coming, yet not knowing whether he might be watching me anyway, from the edge of the woods. It began to grow chilly -- the Bartlebaugh key was icy between my breasts. Irritated, the tequila bringing out my belligerence, I pulled my shirt over my shoulders and lay down, to hell if he was watching.

I must have fallen asleep. Next thing I knew, I felt eyes on me and I opened mine. He stood over me, in his jeans and open shirt. We stared at each other. This time he was not smiling, yet he was still soft, no hardness, no threat. I was lying on my side, toward the fire. He held a walking stick like mine and very slowly caught my shirt collar with the end of the stick and pushed it from my shoulders. He walked around the edge of the circle of light, behind me. I felt his gaze like heat as it moved from the top of my head across my shoulders, into my waist, along my hip and buttocks, down my outer thigh to the backs of my knees down to the soles of my feet. His feet shifted slightly in the grass behind me. I turned over on my back slowly and stared up at the sky. All the stars, and a slice of moon. In the breeze I felt the skin around my clitoris opening. I looked down and saw my nipples had hardened. I closed my eyes. Something of -- shame? bewilderment? -- *his* nipples hadn't hardened when I looked at them last night. His penis hadn't lifted to me. Yet here I lay, everything about me hard and aching. Hungry. Again, hungry. As I had always been, all of my life, hungry.

He moved around to my feet and stood, staring into my face, down my breasts, my belly with its hair, my clitoris (peeping, I was sure, insistent), my dark-haired thighs, my feet. Then he knelt, half squatting, at my feet, and we stared into each other's eyes. I sat up, leaning on my elbows. He looked down at my nipples and through his open shirt I saw his own nipples tighten. Between his legs I saw a denim bulge. My heart was beating hard, I'm sure

he could see that, and I was burning. I wanted to crawl
toward him, to...

He smiled at me. The sight of his long teeth pulled at
me again. He rose softly, turned, and was gone. I put my
hand to my mouth. To my horror I had been about to say
something. "Wait," or "Stop," or "Please." Me, the one
who didn't want us to speak.

I moved through my morning with the unfamiliar
sensation of my nipples brushing erect against my shirt. So
extreme is my reaction to this man that even the laws of
my nature seem to be in aberration. I kept reaching inside
my shirt to touch them, amazed, delighted and somewhat
alarmed at the new feeling, and kept catching myself in
sexual reveries. Envisioning when, where it will happen.
Tonight by the fire again? In the stream? Ranford's
cabin? I let the coffee water boil over, spilled a half pound
of flour. Then I got angry at myself. *Something more,* I
shouted to myself. *Beyond sex,* I throttled myself.

There was nothing to cure it but a noon visit to the
bone room. It had been too many days since I sat in the
white grid. I needed to center myself. All this sexual
preoccupation was exciting, but, like the emptiness after
the euphoria after masturbation, *what for?* So what, if
after twenty-five years of sex, my tits were finally acting
like tits! What good did that do me now? I wondered if
I hadn't been a much happier creature before the doll
maker showed up and started me on this body awareness.
For wasn't that exactly what he had done? The moment
another human entered the picture, centeredness was out
the window. Maybe this was the reason for celibacy vows.
If I had made a vow, then a stranger showing up would not
have this effect, right? There would be rules. Those rules
would govern my responses to him, to the dolls, to his

nudity trips.

Then I got angry at that reaction. I couldn't seem to see this or respond to it in any comfortable way.

I hid my pages under the board in the closet (first looking in paranoia to see he wasn't watching me outside the window), rolled up a blank page, tucked a pencil behind my ear, and walked to Bartlebaugh's, irritated at my nipples bouncing against the fabric.

Again, it was unlocked. *Damn!* There was no escaping! I opened the door and there sat the dollmaker in my white squares, naked, his legs crossed, his back to me, facing the window. He didn't respond to the door opening. I stood a minute, waiting for him to turn. He didn't move.

At first I was angry. I had come to this chapel to get away from him, from thoughts of his nakedness. And here he sat, in my holy place, his clothes piled in a corner.

I had heard about compelling to yourself the thing you seek to avoid, but this was ridiculous.

I did the only thing I could think to do: peeled off my clothes and sat behind him, in the small patch of light his shadow left me. I closed my eyes and crossed my legs with my palms facing up on my knees. Not that I had ever been into yoga, but it had seemed the natural position for meditation, all those afternoons in my bone room. I focused on my breathing and into the center of my forehead until that soft dizziness began and the silence of the room began to ring in my ears. Through all this, the doll maker didn't move or make a sound. He sat, like me, palms up, facing the window. I wanted to laugh at us in our imitation of ritual, but squelched my giggle and focused in seriousness.

Another distraction came: a soft, repeating sound like horses trotting in the distance -- no, like glass, ice tinkling -- I opened my eyes and saw a mobile hanging in the window, made of small, dangling, wooden cubes painted white and a glass crystal in the center, hung on fishing line from a branch, also painted white. It was a hot, still afternoon, but the wooden cubes were light and moved regularly with the faintest breeze at the window. Nice, I thought. Fits the room. Mentally I thanked the mobile-maker; if he had intruded in my chapel, at least he understood where he was and acted accordingly. I closed my eyes again, focusing into breathing, forgetting his presence.

I awoke slumped over, my palms still receptive, my shirt now draped over my shoulders. It must have been about seven; the sun was starting to fade. I guess I fell asleep -- sometimes I do, after meditating. Or meditation becomes sleep -- hard to discern, sometimes. He was gone, I was alone, the door was closed. The mobile still hung in the window. Nothing had been disturbed, the skeletons as I have always had them, the cobwebs intact.

So here I sit with my sheet of paper, my pencil, distracted by the mobile as I try to stare out the window. He is definitely leaving his mark all over my town, changing the quality of my experience. This is what humans do: affect one another. By their mere presence.

In meditation this evening the vision of my mother hitting my right breast returned. In the vision, the tea maker came, silently, his eyes fixed on mine as if telling me to watch. He firmly moved my mother's hand aside just as it was about to make slow motion contact with my skin, lifted her wrist high in the air and pushed her gently back behind him where she disappeared. He then reached and held my breast in his left hand, cupping its roundness carefully. With his other hand he reached between my legs and his fingers began to probe upward into my vagina. I gasped -- I believe I even physically reacted to this vision, sitting sharply upright on the bone room floor. I began to break inside, flooding warm, joyous, splitting. I looked into his eyes as his hand reached further, upward through my womb, his whole arm now up inside of me, reaching into my intestine, the coolness of contact an interior shock. Up under my ribcage, his wrist brushed my heart, throwing the pattern of the beat, undoing all the rhythms, rearranging my cells, disconnecting the old connecting tissue. His fingers probed until they found the inner mammary mass. His eyes fixed on mine as if saying, "This is not a violation, it is an exploration," and then his inner and outer hands touched fingertips and closed around the full sphere of my breast. He sighed, as if relieved at the discovery, closed his eyes, leaned his head against my shoulder, and wrapped his torso and legs around mine. We remained thus until I came to from my meditation. When I opened my eyes and remembered the vision, my eyes began to cry involuntarily. I felt faint, my ears rang, the insides of my body felt bruised in that good aching way the body feels after love-making, and all of me tingled alive.

It had been a healing, I realized. He had needed, desired and insisted on finding the shape of my breast, the essence of what it really is -- a circle, a sphere. He had not just responded to it as a photo image in *Playboy*. This made reparation for my mother's hatred of it, her trying to push it back -- what else is a slap but a pushing back in fast motion? -- for her not wanting to see it, to acknowledge it, either in herself or in her daughter. And it forgave my own self-hatred, my own separation from myself.

I felt bewildered, amazed, silenced. Has he come here for more purposes than I realized? Or am I in a process of healing myself, through him? He knew nothing of the vision. I healed myself, using the image of his hands. That must be it.

◇   ◇

I am rested and relaxed from my meditation, from the sleep, and feel no urgency about when/if I will see him again. That he left without -- well, that is not true. I started to say he left without speaking, but, of course, he senses the rules and would not speak. I can't say he left without a gesture, because, as he pulled off my shirt last night with his walking stick, today he draped it back over my shoulders with his hands. A gesture of -- concern? gentleness? It must have been late when he left, close enough to evening that he felt I would get cold.

I wonder where he sleeps? No, I don't really want to know. That is his secret. It occurs to me that perhaps he hasn't intruded, hasn't been in my cabin or spying on me. That doesn't seem his nature. The ability to be in here, silent, meditating together, the gentle white gesture (I feel it is a white gesture -- everything in this room is white, except for the brown tones of the skins piled in the wardrobe behind me) of draping my shirt over my shoulders -- those are not the movements of an intruder or voyeur. He accepts my presence. Therefore I accept his. And sex may have nothing to do with it -- if, that is, my hunger doesn't interfere. After all, I have to remember that he comes here directly from back there. *He* has not necessarily been without sex for four years. He probably has a wife or lover back there. The encounters by the fire -- if they were anything other than a dream in the first place -- may have been purely curiosity, exposing our vulnerability, proving we have no concealed weapons. Not a sexual thing. Except, of course, my own reaction, which is sexual. But, again, it's been four years, and he is a lovely, lovely...

...my god, only minutes from my waking, here in my white, holy place, and I am thinking of him in that way again. Maybe it is the writing that does this to me. Maybe I would be OK if I stopped the writing. But I can't now. It's all connected, the writing, him, and I must try to keep open. To decide it is or isn't sexual is not keeping open. To decide anything about what this is, is not keeping open.

I need to keep the peace this meditation gave me. I am going to roll up this paper, go back to my cabin, and enjoy the evening. Fix my tea, roll out some biscuits for tomorrow. Maybe even a midnight swim. Not expecting anything, not making any movements any differently than I usually do, alone.

Just these few lines before sleep.

At the stream tonight, as I came up from underneath, I saw him step into the water at the other bank. He saw me, did not react, dove to the bottom, surfaced and swam a bit. Then he floated on his back. I took his cue at first and ignored -- tried to -- his presence, swimming on my side of the stream, careful not to cross the invisible line we had set up. Occasional lightning in the distance silhouetted trees and fireflies edging the stream, green blinking lights. The soft lapping of the water quieted me. A bat swooped silently through the air between us. After a while, I just moved my arms in slow circles and watched him floating, smiling to myself, imagining we were two pale greenish-white frogs pulsing with the night, less aware of our selves than of being gently held up in this life by the dark water and night air. For once, my hunger did not take over, my lust kept its place. I was childishly content to simply watch him, and he simply allowed it. In the quarter moonlight it was easier to see him if I looked a little above his body, a little above the water's surface. The softness of him like that pulled at me. At something other than my hunger. For once it felt like...I don't know...some other thing was happening. To watch and be allowed to. Like when cats let you stroke them. He turned in the water, he let me see his body at rest from every angle. And when he stepped out of the water, picked up his clothes and walked into the woods, he did so as if he was alone. No preening, no moment of macho or boy.

I almost wish I had brought to myself the macho or boy kind of male animal. This one is too -- interesting. Too distracting. But what am I saying? That I prefer the wham-bam-thank-you-ma'am encounter? Jong's zipless? As I said before, a purely physical thing?

No. I do not. That I know.

But I can't name it. Whatever it is I *do* want.

This, what is happening with the tea maker, must be what I want. It is so puzzling, so indefinable.

Coming back to my cabin from the stream, I felt both filled and aching. Oh, I know myself so well, my conditioned sexual self. She is still with me, and with a vengeance. Solitude has not quieted her, has only increased her appetites. A part of me wants the raw, physical encounter with him, and thinks of it constantly now. This trust he demonstrates, these qualities of grace and humor, that he is a human with whom I can coexist peacefully, if not comfortably -- they are a little miracle in my ghost town. And yet I ache for more. All the while so sure -- from experience -- that if we were to couple, this other quality of encounter would change or cease. Something else would happen then, and whatever it would be, I would be left here, in my ghost town, with embittered memories. It would no longer be my own simple place, just me and the dust of other people's yesterdays. Now it would hold the dust of him. Particles of his skin, dust he brought here from his real world home. All mingling, forever. It would become "the cabin we made love in," "the bone room we were silent in," If I let him into my body, he leaves his scent on everything I touch after. And when he leaves -- for he must and will -- I will be struggling in new hungers, ancient hungers. Those exact hungers I came here to escape!

I am so exhausted. The swim, the day. I must sleep.

◇ ◇

I awoke this morning from a dream of fish. In the dream -- and this *was* only a dream, no uncertainty this time -- the man walked toward me in the stream until the water reached his hips. Then his penis, an erect silver fish, glided toward me, breaking the water, pulling his body behind it. I looked into his eyes as the fish came to me, as its mouth first pressed into my belly. The man's eyes were sad, as if he could not control the fish, but wanted to. I awoke.

On my doorstep, a few moments later, a new carving. I picked it up. It was a fish, long, sleek, painted silver. It made me laugh. How far this has come so fast! Four days ago this would have terrified me. Today it makes me laugh, that he knows my dream. I set it on the window, horizontally, between the man and the woman.

◇ ◇

This all feels so familiar. And yet, not at all.

I stayed in my cabin today. Mostly stared at the ceiling beams, the triangular cobwebs stretched into corners. It rained most of the day, grey sheets of rain, the constant falling, falling. Cleansing the world, cleansing the ancient dust in my ghost town, rearranging it into new configurations. Like the raked sand gardens of Japan.

I stood in the back doorway, staring out into the woods. All my windows were open, and the front door, to let in the sharp-scented rain air.

I turned and he was here, standing behind me. He was soaked, his clothes dripping puddles around him, his wet hair stuck to his skull in little points, making him look comical and, therefore, vulnerable. Droplets even fell from his eyebrows to his lip and chin. His eyes were as they had been in the dream. He stood, hunched, a gesture of apology. In the intensity of his gaze -- hazel eyes, like mine -- a sadness, yet an assurance that he had done what I wished in coming here. He had been pulled here by the silver fish.

I took his hand, the tea/doll/mobile/fish maker's hand, with its high veins and deep bones. I met his sorrow with my own sense that we had failed somehow. Yet, inside of me, a tea cup breaking, the warm liquid again. I pulled him into my bedroom. We undressed. I quickly, opening out my sleeping bag to accommodate two; he slowly, staring at his carvings as he did so. He went to the window and laid the dolls down, leaned the fish up vertically between them against the glass. He turned to me, waiting on the bed, his sad eyes laughing.

He lay down next to me. The thick humidity of the rain intensified his scents -- from the hair under his arms, cumin and russian olive; from the hair at his penis, camomile and brie. These scents assured me I would be fed. I could not breathe normally, was almost hyper-ventilating, as if I had jumped into cold water. Only it was warm water, bubbling and chilling hot up my thighs, simply at the presence of his scents in my bed. We reached for each other's faces and hair, our fingers moving softly over lips and eyelids, tracing the pink shells of our ears, holding out strands of hair and smiling at the realization that they were not grey but silver. Our eyes and mouths moved through soundless mimes of amazement,

joy, laughter and infinite sorrow -- a momentary flash of
sadness, as we realized the ultimate insufficiency of body
language to express the inexpressible. Then, staring into
each other's eyes, we began to laugh, softly, and pulled
closer, entwining our legs, his feet prehensile, caressing
my calves. His was a low laugh, softly nubbed like a
sunwarmed adobe wall under my fingers. The texture and
color of our pubic hair was the same. No fantasies, no
posing. He was a hungry man, and my body with its
rough hair pleased him. Once I was sure of that -- when
he laughed low, rubbed his face in my belly hair, and
playfully tugged on the hair of my thighs -- I lost any trace
of reluctance. With urgency I pulled him toward me,
moaning and burrowing my nose into his different gardens
of hair, inhaling deeply the unique scents of each dark,
folded place. His scents were so intoxicating they had to
be foreign, yet I had known what they would be. His skin
was not really that of a new lover, but familiar, as if we
had been lovers once, years ago.

As in my meditation vision, he focused his gaze on
mine and we lay still, our arms entwined, and we became
lost -- no, found -- in each other's eyes. His face seemed
to move and change, became older, younger, showed itself
to me as it had been and would or might be, at different
points in his evolution. Fear, innocence, vulnerability,
masking, cunning, cruelty, joy -- his face continually
transformed as I stared into his eyes, which stayed in the
present and did not change.

He reached for my right breast and I drew a sharp
breath. My vision? His left hand moved down my belly
to my clitoris and his fingers began to massage in small
circles which grew larger until my entire belly moved in
the circle he created. Then with both hands he cupped my
breast, his eyes telling me to watch, to be aware of what

would come next. He lowered himself slowly so that his head was level to my nipple, and pulled it toward his lips. At that moment I felt he claimed it, took it to himself, for his purposes, as no man had ever done before. As the tea maker began to suckle me, sensation stirred deep within the center of the sphere, and moved up through my nipple to his lips and tongue and teeth. I gasped and my body tensed. If viewed from above the bed my movements were fearful, yet I followed by pushing my nipple deeper into his mouth, pushing my body urgently against his. The sensation quickly became one of pain. He held my breast tightly, pulling and kneading it like bread until it seemed to lose its original shape. I thought I felt him break the skin and drink from the nipple. I was certain, in fact, that milk was pouring out of me -- I who had never made babies or milk -- into his mouth, down his throat. It frightened me; this did not fit into any plans or expectations of sexuality for me, but I pushed past the fear. I wanted to feel what this was, to find out where it would go, what would happen next. As if he knew I ached for extreme sensations, he was audacious with my breast, as male, as child, as animal. As he drank from me, his legs -- thick thighs like huge warm arms -- curled around mine, up over my hips, across my spine, in necessity, in contentment. He kept one hand on my breast and with the other reached around to my back, to my waist, and pulled me toward him insistently, pulling me closer with his legs and arms, sucking deeply. I looked down at his greying head, at his eyes closed. Was this sensation maternal? Was he a child to me? No, he was a man, a man with greying hair, moving into his aging time. He was drinking with insistence at his right to it, with clear assertion of his knowledge that this was what we both wanted. As no one had ever done. I became lost as he moved his hands to touch my thighs, my ass, between my legs, exploring gently everywhere.

I had never been so aware of internal momentary changes as my body prepared to receive him. Amazed as a child, I felt my vagina as it changed and hollowed, making the place for the tea maker's penis to enter. Barometric changes, gathering up of tree branches before they hurl outward like arms in a storm, the pulling upward, intake of breath before pushing outward, exhaling the love cry. I felt his penis pulse in my hand, it moved like a small animal, chameleon, many colors. Here the artist learned to paint skin tone with every color imaginable, that it was not simply "pink," not the crayola "flesh" color. Purple, green, blue, red, yellow, brown, this multicolored miracle. As it grew larger -- (amazed, I watched -- How could this be? It was this size and has somehow become this other size -- Although I never looked away, although it changed as I watched, how is it I was not allowed to see the cells pushing against each other for the changing? Sleight of hand, in my hand, sly silk.) -- I realized the thick veins of it were the same bluegreen swelling on the backs of his hands, those artist's veins arched to shape and render the visible. On his penis, veins arched to shape and render the invisible, inside of me. As I traced with my fingers and eyes the particular shape of him, I felt my vagina walls change in correspondence, opening and reforming cells into the exact necessary mold for his penis. Not just "a penis," but this penis, of this man, this moment. I reached inside to feel, his fingers followed mine, to see what we had made, in our expectation. We waited again, falling into each other's eyes, our hands stopped, sweet and sticky, on each other's thighs. Then he lowered his legs from the edge of the bed, pulled my legs toward his hips, and held my hips firmly there while pushing slowly, opening me. A chaos of perfect order as he came inside.

I heard myself singing, a high unfamiliar note. Giving and receiving were one total, complete and same movement. I opened my eyes to watch his face as I felt the turgidity that meant he was about to ejaculate inside of me. And, to my joy, his features did not twist into the accustomed repressed agony, anger, hatred and resentment I had seen on the faces of other men. The tea maker's face opened first in bewilderment, amazement, then laughter. He was open, he could lose himself without the fear, without resenting his need, without the holding back. It was not the expected noise, from his throat, of relinquishment despite oneself, but a cry of one who finds himself falling and chooses instead to fly, a cry of willing embrace of loss of the known. We spoke together then, our only vocalizations the entire afternoon, besides the laughing. We cried and sang, coyote cries, cries of feline and canine, of hunger pouring over into thirst into feeding into a satiation that only compelled a deeper hunger. We moved until impetus and reaction became indiscernible, the need to move, the movement, countermovement, all became one.

We died into small naps, awoke to chilled shoulders and thunder, moved together like babies for warmth, then fed in the dark rain, dying again, waking...like ocean waves, resisting, then pulling. Against the dark cold, the fevered smells of our feast filled the room, cumin, warm sugar and cheese. Once I woke to the sound of the wind in the trees, the constant grey motion of the water around the cabin, and had the sensation that we slept in a timeless cave deep under the ocean, the soft vibration of water's movement slapping against our walls. It was a simultaneous sense of intense danger and unthreatened security. I held him closer, breathed him in deeply, and slept again.

The white spider web came somewhere in the middle

of the afternoon, maybe the third time we awoke. I was in that place so deep into the body I was out of body. My eyes opened, then closed to fully concentrate on a sensation of white, wet strings that, in my sleep, had begun to move outward from me, radiating from my vulva to his fingers. Cool slivers stretched along my thighs and belly, across the sleeping bag, a shimmering cat's cradle in his fingers which danced lightly against my skin, as he leaned over me, a magician, an artist, lost in his creation. As I came awake I was confused, but drugged into not caring -- did the strings start from his fingers or from inside of me? I felt their color, their silky white texture. It was a glistening web, or I was a web, or he was a web. Or one of us was a spider. Or we created a spider together. My face was fixed in astonished joy. The loss of space and time, the loss of him and the loss of me. The sleeping and the love washed in and out of each other so that the memory of it is soft, grey, wet and never clear. The memory and my body share a secret.

That had never happened for me in civilization, even with all the intensity of my hungers there. In civilization we were only animals; sex was the place we could cry out against the constraints of walking upright during the day, against the concrete. Here in my ghost town, there were no walls to rage against, no guttural cry to assert, no need to prove our genesis. Being animals here was a given, not a pose or a momentary lapse. Yet we knew no separation from spirit, we were talon as well as light, the weight-lessness of evaporation as certainly as the pressure of bone and skin. We were one creature, separations of male and female forgotten, an undulation, pure motion. I can't imagine such a merging ever happening in a city, in an apartment high in the air, with a television on in the next room, air-conditioning, polyester sheets.

◇   ◇

I awoke in the night of the ocean and he was gone. I had expected that. How else? That was when I got up and wrote about it.

Today, the day after, my body aches, inside, outside. The thin outer layer of skin on my right nipple is rough under my finger, small tears, and the center of the nipple is circled with tiny purple teeth marks and red swellings. I imagine the earth aches with me, after all the pressure of rain. The trees, soaked, now drying, stretch against the drying. My spirit also aches. I feel weighted, sad, grey. It is still dark today, another overcast day. And humid, a condition rare here. All the rain from yesterday is swelling the ground. My windows won't budge to shut or open, their wooden frames are swollen.

I have spent the whole day here, inert. On the bed, staring at the cobwebs again.

◇   ◇

He didn't come last night.

I dreamed of him, though. I dreamed he came and we sat like buddhas, face to face on my bed. I traced with my eyes, memorizing as if for one last time, the soft hairiness of his stomach skin, the deep V of his belly, the cone and egg, sphere, line and ellipse of his penis and scrotum soft, hot and cool, at rest. His calves and thighs swelling, pressed against each other, sweat forming in the crease behind his knees, and in the crease where his legs joined his pelvis. There also my memory lingered, the strong sweet smell there. I stared at his feet, the soft little spheres of his toes, the white arch, soft clay of him, seeing all the places he had walked, the streams at which he had stopped to wash his feet, and all the places he would walk in leaving here. We touched hands, lightly, and stared into each other's eyes. There was a sadness so intense I heard myself sob. One sound, escaping from my throat, the second verbal sound I had made in several days. I usually talk to myself here in my town. Not lately, not since I've known I'm not alone. When I cried in the dream, he touched my lips, a gesture of silence. But his eyes were filled with knowing why I cried. Then I awoke.

I no longer doubt that he is real.

He took the dolls. After the ocean, when I awoke the next morning, the window sill was empty. And an odd thing -- I hadn't dusted in here for several days, too preoccupied to be my usual orderly self...when I touched the window where the dolls had been, I left a fingerprint. Yet there were no prints from the dolls. As if they had never been here. Again, like the teapot in Ranford's cabin. Strange. It saddened me that he took them. But I understood why. The dolls were images of our selves before the ocean. No longer applicable. The fish was also gone. It had offered connection in a dream. Now we were connected in dreams and in waking. The fish no longer necessary. The carvings had been like words between us. No longer valid now, they faded as words do. Something else had happened to take their place.

For the first time since his arrival, the bone room was locked. So still inside, stuffy, the window swollen shut from the rain. I've been sitting, facing the window, trying to focus, but can't. All I'm doing is waiting to hear his footsteps. Although I've never heard them before. He has always simply appeared, without a sound.

The mobile is gone, too. That saddens me, more than the dolls and fish. The mobile was correct in here. The sound of bones clicking together was right for the room, for the meditation. I should fashion one myself, of the bits of vertebrae in this room, and fishing line. I will do that.

Guess I'll go back to my cabin.

I'm beginning to wish it had gone differently. When
he came into my cabin, I should have just fixed us tea.
We should have sat, silently, watching the storm together,
perhaps our eyes meeting in laughter, in memory of that
day he stood naked at the edge of the woods. Perhaps we
could have spoken in sign language; touching the teapot for
more tea, leading him by the hand to the dolls in the
window, touching them together.

Suddenly it occurs to me, we *did* have a conversation
without words. What else had our touching, the entering
of each other, been? Does anything more need to be said?
Or done?

Perhaps it isn't regret I'm feeling as much as fear.
What has happened between me and this man is so close to
feeding the deepest hungers I have ever had, that I'm afraid
to trust that it could actually happen, afraid it could only
happen in my imagination. Not having seen him since the
ocean night, and the dolls being gone, I can't help but
wonder again if I made him up. So hard to keep in mind
that it doesn't matter -- that perhaps it doesn't matter
whether such communication happens in the real flesh-and-
blood world, between men and women, as long as it is
imaginable. Isn't it said that anything a human can
imagine, a human can do? Usually that's said in reference
to the worst of our capacities, not the highest. I have
always had this belief that the sexes could communicate,
coexist at a much higher order, accomplish so much more
together. It was partly that belief which led me to this
ghost town, away from the world where I felt inept to
achieve it myself.

No, it is imaginable, but not possible. Either this has
been a figment of my sunburnt imagination (A mirage,

perhaps? An oasis to my drying sexuality?) or the backpacker's version of a one night stand. If he and I were to actually talk and share history, we might find ourselves ridiculously incompatible!

If I could only let go my idealistic vision, go back to society, find a compatible, companionable male, get married, write novels about my ideals and make a living off my dreams. Instead, I hide away in this ghost town, trying to live a dream that, actually, can't be achieved by hiding, singularly. It requires the presence of at least one other human. Damn! Until this man came here, I was content not to have my dream, satisfied enough to hide away from the world that would not allow me that dream. Now I am neither content to stay here, nor able to go back.

I must talk to him. I must find out if I have been correct, if our sharing has been. . .

Then it has *not* been what I thought. If it were, the trust would go without saying. So to speak. Or not.

◇   ◇

I don't think he's coming back. I feel that he has left my town. My ghost has haunted me and now is gone.

The carvings are gone, as if they never existed. Even the Ranford cabin teapot. I looked there, on my way back to my cabin this afternoon, and it's no longer in the cabinet. Would he really carry a china teapot in a backpack?

Again, the thoughts about reality, sanity, fantasy. At some moments it doesn't matter to me. Other times, like now, it feels crucial that I know.

6. The Tea Ceremony

Raining again. Or still. It hasn't stopped all day. It is dusk now. I am writing by the light of my Jar Bottom candle, violating one of my few rituals by keeping it burning on a non-holiday, and not really caring if I burn it to the bottom. So this is what happens to rituals when they outlive their origins. I once inherited a set of expensive china cups with gold rims and holly painted on them. I let myself drink out of them daily, but never could let go a vague feeling of unease. There would be no sense of ritual, no bringing them out, dusting them off for Christmas eggnog. Abused daily, with coffee, milk, tea, juice. I even watered kitchen plants with them. Defiance against my ancestors and their special china behind glass, only used for special occasions, increasing in value.

So even in my ghost town some perverse part of me must violate rituals, even when there are none externally imposed. It is that same part of me which brought me here in the first place. That same part of me which brought *him* here. What is more perverse than to disrupt one's own solace with a phantom of one's own making? I don't at all like what I've done. This having him appear behind my back in my own cabin and leading him to my bed. This irreplaceable ocean, this never-to-be-repeated perfect sexual union, this healing which leaves me aching and lost in my eternal, quiet ghost town. *Perverse.* I want to undo it. It goes against everything I was trying to explore. Yet it is simply what happened, despite me, a kind of flow, not planned, as I said it would be. Is there an organic "plan," a kind of logical shape, when two of the opposite sex are brought together? This is what I must know. *Is* it unavoidable? *Is* it "human nature," an unchangeable thing?

I think back to a mentor I had, the same one who told me not to write in the first person. We never could agree on the endings of my stories. The fictions I wrote under his tutelage were about male/female relationships. He swore at me for pulling two people together in a story and then "not letting the inevitable happen," not "giving the readers what you've led them to expect." I put those stories away in folders, never finished, where they collected dust and time. Years later I pulled them out, impressed with the writing, not recognizing the plots, reading them as if new, as if written by another hand. And my mentor's notes, his irritated, exasperated, red margin notes. Still, after the passing of years and the severing of our mentor relationship, I was still unable to either agree or disagree with him. For it made it one kind of story if they came together, and then...went apart? Of course, went apart, for I was writing "serious literature" and happy endings were for housewives' magazines. It made another kind of story if they longed for each other, but never quite came together. I spent an evening on the floor of my study, poring over those aborted fictions, those men and women forever caught in space and time, almost touching, never quite... I was depressed for days. It was soon after that that I had the call about my father's illness, pulled the map to my ghost town from his file, tucked it into my suitcase, and made my decision.

I could rework it, rewrite this one. Coming here has been no escape from my concerns, has only delayed my confronting them. I have hopefully simplified the process, brought it down to one woman, one man, and, even more simple, a scenario in which I have total control.

I stopped for a long time, staring at those last four words. They wavered, danced in the light of my Jar Bottom candle, lifting and falling from the page. Mocking me. Maybe I should take my mentor's advice. Go back to the rules. Starting with the third person.

Where was she, before he entered her cabin? She was standing in a rain storm. Like this one, that continues. Staring out the back door, all her windows and front door open to let in the sharp, clean air. Like they are now. Only it was mid-afternoon then. It is night now. Perhaps vision at night will be more true.

So what happens now? The silver wooden fish sits in the window with the other dolls. She stands, staring, half hoping to see him in the woods, through the rain... (go back, pull the pages from the floorboard, find the exact words)...

> *He stood, hunched, a gesture of apology. In the intensity of his gaze -- hazel eyes, like mine -- a sadness, yet an assurance that he had done what I wished in coming here. He had been pulled here by the silver fish.*

Well, that rips it. The last sentence, pulled here by the silver fish. Now what do I do? Look into his eyes, shake my head sadly, gently escort him to the door, back into the rain? Do I push him into a chair, pour him a cup of tea? Do we sit, silently, staring past each other out two windows, letting the soft light of the afternoon fade quickly to grey, then to dark, and still sit, silently, staring past each other?

Maybe if I go into the bedroom now, lie down by myself, I can -- recreate the scene?

No, no, no. There is no recreating it anyway. I will go in, lie down, see what comes.

The candle is still burning. After all, I've only lit it for ten minutes at a time, only four times in four years. It has an entire candle life reserved in it, all to burn in one night.

I went into the bedroom to lie down. As I sat on the edge of the bed, a shock ran through me: on the window sill, the dolls had returned. The woman, the fish, the man. As they had been before, the man and woman standing, the fish horizontal. As if the man had never come here, had never moved them, had never *re*moved them.

I thought I might be losing my mind. I rubbed my eyes, but the dolls were still there after the blurring cleared. Either he had never been here at all, or he had returned, perhaps this afternoon when I was out, and replaced them. My own fashioning of events and time might explain his never having been here at all. That I could deal with -- on one level -- but if he had returned the dolls this afternoon, then I was completely bewildered. What, then, had his taking them away meant? What did his returning them mean?

All afternoon I had a sense that something was different. That he was, perhaps, gone. Or had never been here, or that he was not to return again. An emptiness, a dryness. But with the rain, the swelling again of the wood of my cabin, the breaking of that thing in the ground that gave off that sharp, hopeful smell, I had let myself hope he

might be back, there might be more...
...I seemed to know, only a few hours ago, where this
was heading. Now I am lost, bewildered. Either he came
and we made love. Or he never came and we never made
love.
But, wait, I thought, going to the window, touching the
fish. Aren't there two other possibilities? That he perhaps
was here but we never made love? Or that he was never
here and we did make love? If I was to be open, as I had
vowed I would be at the beginning of this journal, then I
had to consider those alternatives. I had to consider all
possible alternatives, all *im*possible alternatives, and
alternatives I couldn't even imagine.
In the middle of these lunatic ravings -- (for it *was*
lunatic, to preoccupy myself with these rationalizations in
the midst of the most irrational experience I had ever had.
The secret, I had yet to learn, was to silence my thinking
mind, the part of me that wanted to explain everything, to
eliminate the need for explanation) -- I smelled the
unmistakable scent of tea. Not ordinary black tea, the kind
in the pot on my wood stove, but *jasmine* tea. Flowers,
perhaps, outside the window, their scent opened in the
rain? But there were no jasmine flowers outside my
window or anywhere near my ghost town. The smell came
from my sitting room. It was a warm, steaming smell. I
turned slowly, wondering, and went to the bedroom door.

He sat there -- no, here, in this chair in which I now
sit. He sat pouring steaming water from my kettle into his
cream china pot with red flowers. Next to the tea pot were
two cups. Unfamiliar cups. One of very old, very thin,
almost translucent, china, pale blue. The other a bright
yellow cup, modern, thick, mug-shaped. A chill went
through me as I realized that he sat in front of my

manuscript as he poured the tea water. As I watched, transfixed, a drop of kettle water fell onto my pages of butcher paper. He daubed at the water spot with his shirt sleeve and continued pouring, carefully, with concentration. Time had slowed, like the slowed movements in a film. The water from the kettle seemed endless, and the tea pot bottomless. The movements of his arms and shoulders were slow, graceful, haunting. It seemed such a long time that I stood in the doorway, staring, watching the water flow from kettle to tea pot. I let myself look at his face. He was unaware of me, completely, as he had been that day in the Ranford cabin. Total concentration on the tea water. Next to his elbow, my Jar Bottom candle flickered, but even its light moved slowly, uncannily slow for a candle sitting in the window's draft. The air moved against my skin more gently than it had earlier, tiny pummelings, minute proddings against the hairs on my arms, gentle, the coolness slowed and saturating my skin. A tingle of joy went through me, and it, too, moved lingeringly, taking forever to move from my throat to my toes. The colors of the room: the golden light from the wood stove, from the candle, the fading sunset through the window. Suddenly we were at dusk again, earlier, not the darkness that had descended while I was in the bedroom. I could see the horizon, turning my head to look out to the woods from the back door, flashing slow and hot pink as double streaks of lightning shot down, white gold against red pink. With the intake of my breath, my throat burned. Everything had slowed and intensified.

It began to rain, soundlessly, and I felt a compulsion to rush outside, run through the water, drench myself. I heard a sob pass my lips and I fell to my knees in the doorway. For I was now at the back door, in the room with him, staring out at the rain and woods, feeling him behind me, still, pouring the tea water. Forever pouring the tea water at my table with my words forever exposed to his eyes. As soon as he would put down the kettle, as soon as the tea pot was filled, then time would settle back into itself, the pink sky would ink to black again -- with a tinge of purple -- the Jar Bottom candle would flicker and die. He would set the kettle back on the stove, light a kindling twig from the wood stove fire, and relight the candle, setting it away from the draft. He would begin to read my butcher paper as the jasmine flowers steeped at his elbow. I would lean against the old wood of my doorway, watching him read. After a time, he would look up at the tea kettle...

...looked up at the tea kettle. Still not at me. As if I was not present, was invisible to him. He closed his eyes, inhaling the jasmine steam as he poured first the yellow cup, then the blue. He pushed the blue cup carefully toward the edge of the table, toward where I stood, yet as if he still didn't see me there. He wrapped his veined hands around his yellow mug and continued reading. I watched the steam rise from the frail blue cup. The scent was irresistible, sharpened by the rain. My left shoulder and arm were chilled and wet from the doorway and I was shaking from the cold. I went to the table slowly, making no noise with my feet, and sat cautiously across from him. I stared at my blue cup of tea, not at his face. The china was so thin, so fragile, why didn't it melt from the tea heat? I touched the rim. Scalding hot. I pulled back my finger and held it with my other hand. The heat was real.

He continued to read, as if I was not present. I closed my eyes. His scent filled the air directly behind the jasmine scent, that strong, male cat scent, again the scent of unwashed cotton. I sucked it in slowly, inhaling as hard as I could, and his scent filled me, a slow rush through my veins. A kind of meditation, to breathe in his scent, hold it, then let it escape with an anguished parting. I inhaled it again, held it, then let it go. I opened my eyes. His were staring directly into mine. From under the eyebrows, from under the line of his skull. No emotion. No recognition. No reaction. We stared.

I don't know how long we stared. I had to close my eyes against it, finally. It was too strong. Too much being said, too much not being said, and none of it translated into the rational. Although I had left the rational behind, I could not guarantee for how long before it would invade me again and have to be expelled.

I reached for the tea cup then, keeping my eyes closed. Warm, not scalding. I lifted it and drank the flower water. It was sweet, both light and heavy at once, with a pleasant bark-bitter aftertaste. I settled my blue cup back in its saucer, then opened my eyes.

He was gone.

The tea pot was there. The two cups. The candle flickering. But the man was gone. I sat still, a shock passing through my shoulders, down my spine. His scent was still there, faint, receding. Then gone entirely. I touched the tea pot. Cold. I put my finger in my tea cup. Cold. Only seconds ago I had drunk the hot liquid. Now cold.

I sat there for a long time, unable to think, or feel, or move. Unable to say what had happened. Finally I stood, walked to the front door, and looked out onto the street. The rain had stopped. All around me water dripped from the trees, splashed out through the gutter on my roof, and slapped into the buckets in my cabin. Nothing to be seen. I went to the back door, stared out into the woods. No movement there. I went into my bedroom. The dolls were gone. Again. I turned back to the other room. The tea pot was gone. The yellow cup. The blue one. The fire had died in the wood stove and the room was cold. The Jar Bottom candle had guttered out.

It was dark and cold and alone in my cabin.

Stoking the fire, I stared into it as it built itself back up. I closed the doors and windows against the cold, lit the candle once again, and stood over the pages of butcher paper. The last words written there were "I will go in, lie down, see what comes..."

Over the words, "see what comes", the ripple of a now dried tea stain. The pencil there smeared and darkened.

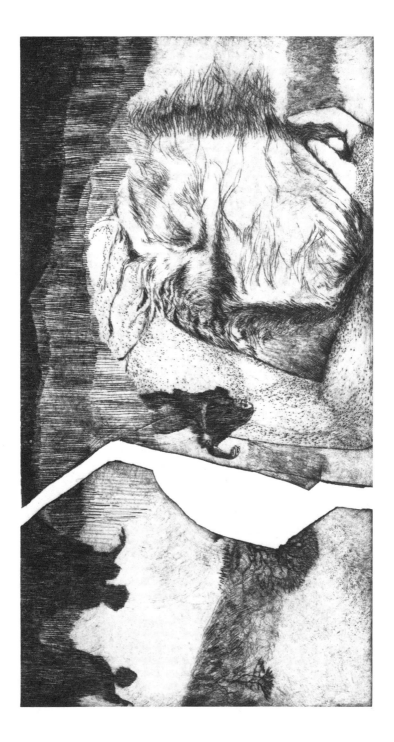

7. The White Grid

This is the last of the butcher paper left on the roll. I'm not sure what happens after this. Perhaps I will follow my idea of writing on the walls of the cabins, A whole other sort of experience can come of that. Writing directly over ancient fingerprints, wiping dust that has clung tenaciously for eighty years. Perhaps not even use the pencils, write with the eraser tip, tracing the letters into the dust. Undoing what I write as I write it. Leaving it, until, in another eighty years, my words are lost, entirely dusted over.

I am in the bone room once again. It is now three days since the evening of what I ironically call "the tea ceremony." There has been no sign of my visitor. The bone room was still locked when I came here the next day. In the past three days I have felt a kind of giddiness about daylight and sanity, a kind of relief and release that he has not come again. I admit the first night I waited, conscious that he might be watching me outside my cabin, seeing me framed in my windows. And fought that with the same anger with which I had fought the store windows. Windows. They serve an unavoidable function, whether glassed or not. They allow limited, framed, posed visions.

93

Versions. Either of ourselves, by ourselves, or by someone else. I begin to resent them. If it weren't for wanting to let in the sunlight and moonlight and breezes, I'd board them over entirely.

By the second night I felt alone. No sense of his presence in my town, no sense of sudden possible intrusion. Yet, a few minutes ago, when I came here to the bone room to write these words on the last sheet of butcher paper, the mobile was back. The white twig and white cubes and crystal. It made me laugh. I still am confident that he has not been here, that he left after the tea ceremony. In whatever manner, the same as he came. I suspect the mobile is a gift from myself to myself. I am still going to make the one with vertebrae, though. There needs to be a permanent one, one I make with my own physical hands. I certainly can't count on this one remaining. Not necessarily. Whimsical fragment.

I am ending this the way I began it. Only because the paper has run out, not because this is a proper literary ending place. That was one of the rules: no plans, no outlines, no structure, no storyline to be resolved at the end. I only put endings on my novels because my publisher forced me to. I never did finish those short stories, although my publisher wanted a collection. Now I don't have to listen to anyone's voice in the structured world asking for false, rational endings. I don't have to explain to myself what happened with the man. Oh, of course, there are impulses, throughout the day, to sit down and filter it through, to write an orderly chronology of events and try, from that, to determine the nature of the experience, to extract some rational understanding of it.

I did that all too often with my experiences in the world of people. As if "coming to a conclusion" helped. As if it taught me anything at all. All I learned was that the same memory, as each year went by, took on a different meaning, a different conclusion. And, after a while, I began to *expect* the conclusions to alter, so I could never take as final any momentary interpretation.

I am fighting those impulses to interpret, explain, conclude this sequence of events, or whatever they are.

And simply continue from here. I'm not really sure what I will do next. It will soon be time for a supply run. Perhaps, once I get there, I will decide to stay. For a while.

Or not.

The midday sun is at its perfect moment now. The white light is forming its grid on the floor of this, my perfectly still, untouched chapel. My cobwebs, my bones. This is the only room in town where the cobwebs are white. Everywhere else, they are weighted, brown with dust. The air in this room seems to hold itself, an inhalation never exhaled. Nothing stirs. Nothing changes.

It is so still that the mobile does not make a sound, hangs white in the window, frail, the crystal not even casting a rainbow.

STORIES OF DESIRE AND POWER

Nighthawks

(Oil on Canvas. 1942. Edward Hopper.)

Chelsea's, the bar across from the Hyde Park frame store. Students over pitchers of beer, blue collar men tilting their mugs toward a framed print of Marilyn Monroe. A bar with a history of names and owners, each era having left its contribution to an eclectic assembly of steins, photos of old Chicago, bowling trophies gathered on top of a baby grand, covered with a burgundy fringed throw. Stained glass the only illumination, and the slowly-revolving beer clock over the bar. A place where people watch each other, passively, no one in active pursuit.

A table of three women. Two newcomers approach. The auburn-haired, freckled one with a precocious child's face and brisk, rush-hour gait, twists her arms out of a brown plaid coat, shaking off the light evening snow. The tall, dark-haired woman with a long boy's body glances around the room sharply, quickly observing everyone, yet meeting no one's eyes as she twirls her black cape from her thin shoulders. Her neckline displays a prominent collar bone, a bird's wing across her chest.

The three women seated at the table, although having arrived before these two, seem not as at ease in the bar as these late arrivals. It isn't their neighborhood; they've not been here before. They giggle and point to the bowling trophies. One in a navy pullover stares in fascination at the Marilyn Monroe print behind the bar. Periodically she gazes around the bar, but she keeps coming back to the print, amazed and shocked at the pinkness of the nipples, the tautness of the ribcage thrust

97

forward, the face blatantly in orgasm. After each scanning of the print, the woman lifts her beer. She drinks more energetically than the others at the table.

The two new arrivals settle into their chairs as the auburn-haired one, Merritt, introduces the dark-haired one, Anna, to the first three women. Merritt and these three women work at the museum, but seldom see each other socially. Uncomfortable silences punctuated by giggles. These women have arranged this "girls' night out" in an unimaginative attempt to break past the stiff boundaries of office hierarchy. Merritt has agreed to come to the bar tonight more out of a sense of office politics than keen interest in her coworkers. She has brought Anna along -- her newly divorced friend -- both to expand Anna's social circle and to ensure herself against tedium this evening.

Anna brushes her hair off her face, shaking out snowflakes into her cape hood. She orders a glass of burgundy. Merritt, wiping condensation from her designer glasses on her sleeve, asks for a beer glass and a second pitcher. Merritt and the three women lifting beers together all wear wedding bands. Anna clicks her burgundy goblet to their glasses with a ringless hand.

The conversation continues where it left off. Anna listens. "...and it really struck me, how strange it was. No one there, just the TV. I wanted to order up a drink or something, but it felt weird to do it just for me. Ralph always does, when I go with him on trips. He says, 'How else do you know you're really in a hotel unless you call room service for *some*thing, even just ice?' But I couldn't do it. And then going to breakfast the next day, walking in, sitting alone -- "

"I know. I went alone to Detroit once for a seminar. The worst part is after you've ordered, while you're waiting for your food. I never realized how long you could stretch out adding sugar and cream to your coffee!"

"Or how many words there are to read on a sugar packet!"

The women laugh. Anna smiles softly, remembering another time.

"...anyway, even if they offer me the job, I don't know if I'll take it. So much time alone, away from Ralph. It would just be weird."

"Speaking of TV -- "

"Who's speaking of TV? God, girl, how many have you had?"

"No, Bren just said she watched TV in the hotel -- did you all see *Knot's Landing* last night?"

"Oh, yes -- Anna, don't you just love Michelle Lee?"

"I didn't see it. I don't have a TV."

The three women stare at Anna, curious. Merritt beckons the waitress for popcorn.

"No TV? How do you manage?"

"I -- "

"What do you *do?* God, I tell you, after a day at the museum I just want my dinner on my lap, feet up, and Mary Tyler Moore reruns."

"Oh, she probably doesn't have time for it," says the woman in the navy pullover. "You know these Hyde Parkers. Great Books courses. Shakespeare, DNA lectures. I bet you and your husband spend the evening reading by a proverbial fireplace -- didn't Merritt say you were a potter or something?"

"No, I'm a print maker. And I'm not married. I mean -- I'm divorced."

"You live alone?"

"Yes -- "

"Wow. Don't you get scared?" the woman with the TV asks, staring at Anna.

"Well, yes -- no -- "

"Anna lives in a lovely place at 56th, the sweetest place," Merritt inserts, scooping a fistful of popcorn into her mouth and winking at Anna.

"But 56th *alone?* We live off 53rd -- just last night on the news they showed that woman's body being carried out of that place on 46th and said an average of seven rapes and one murder a week happens over there. There I'm sitting, Joe's at class, and I'm only eight blocks away. It really blew my mind. I was damn glad he was on his way home. I just couldn't live in this area alone."

"Perhaps that's one advantage to not having a TV."

"It's not just this area -- I wouldn't live alone anywhere in this city. I tell you, soon as Ralph's got that degree, we're getting out. Some place small, quiet, a little college town where he can teach. I want a rose garden, damn it!"

"But you'll miss it -- the galleries, the concerts."

"Yeah, that's the clincher. Civilization."

"Anyway, I really admire your courage, Anna."

Anna shrugs, smiles. The conversation moves to children, interdepartmental politics in each woman's husband's field of study, museum staff gossip.

Anna leans her elbow on the table, her chin propped in her hand, pretends to listen, gazing around the room. She sees others like herself, half listening to conversations at their tables, lifting their glasses and exhaling their cigarettes as excuses to survey other tables. Like the man and woman in the Edward Hopper painting, *Nighthawks*. Anna had spent the afternoon at the Hopper Retrospect at the Art Institute and had been mesmerized by his portraits of solitary women in both private and public moments.

All that sun, the women getting into and out of clothing, or nothing to do with clothing, sitting on beds or chairs, standing in windows, unaware of their nakedness, alone, their faces fixed in expectant waiting.

The younger ones in cafes, any minute someone would come in, alleviate their aloneness and transport them beyond cafe cups of tea, silvered radiators of heat.

The older ones, their faces fixed through time's lines into a hopeful waiting, their eyes flat, staring lost into the sun. No longer expecting that anyone would come, that things would change. Some of them having chosen to be alone. In motel rooms, one suitcase. Waiting for inner movement now. Slowed down. But not hopeless; waiting, certain of something more. No longer fixed in their definitions of what that something more would be. Open. But not prime movers.

Some nights Anna was those women. Some nights home from the frame store, her body weary from the hours of tension, the defensive, hunched walk home, the cold. Water whistling from the kitchen, cup rinsed out, tea. In the dark, staring out. Not at sun. At streetlight, at dark. At the empty schoolyard across the street, where she had watched the children change into their Halloween costumes last week, little girls giggling in their tutus.

Other nights, activity. In poor light, until her eyes ached, intricate scratching into the drypoint plate for her print making, of limbs, faces staring out of windows, always looking to the side, out beyond the boundaries of the plate to some possible, fixed, expected world out there.

She began to think the ones to respect were the ones who had learned the reality of aloneness, those who had come to accept it, not with resignation, but as something vaguely irritating to be waved aside. A nagging fly, and business done despite it. Those who had learned to focus away from it into what they did best, into their way of contributing. And the ones most fortunate, to Anna's eyes, were the ones who had found a partner who believed the same, who had a way to contribute, each, to focus away from the nagging fly. Two living together who did not expect each other to erase the essential aloneness. Two who could quell it at times, but did not look to each other to eradicate it. There were those who fought it, focused on it alone in their rooms at night. With tears or TV or beer. And those who, believing it could be cured, mated with others who also believed that myth. And those couples lived their days and nights scratching to get at each other, or scratching each other to get at something else.

Hopper's paintings said all of this to Anna. It was her truth. And she, some nights, scratched against the drypoint plate, against the nagging fly... She would be those solitary Hopper women, she had decided.

◇   ◇

One man in the bar looks interesting to Anna -- mildly so, as a specific point in the room on which to fix her attention. A trick to alleviate the slow softening diffusion the wine is causing in her vision. She becomes aware that the other women at the table, like herself, are becoming listless and that they are aware she is watching the man. Perhaps they feel they inhibit her, the only single woman at their table. And they do. She pulls her attention back to them.

"Well, I've got to be getting home. Joe has a class so it's my night to feed Tommy."

Merritt touches Anna's arm.

"You wanted to show me your new prints?"

The woman with the television looks interested.

"Oh, could I stop by, too? I'd love to see -- " She turns to her friend. "Would you mind, Bren, just a quick look? Then I'll take you home."

"You're all welcome," Anna smiles at them, masking her preference to go home alone. She isn't ready to have strangers in. Her place is minimal, not like her marital home in the suburb, which was always ready for -- indeed, especially created for -- showing, expressing, welcoming.

◇   ◇

Anna hung her cape slowly, straightening the hood on the hanger, to delay witnessing their reactions in the room behind her. To not see what was causing, "Oh, how sweet," "She's so creative, I never would have thought of putting those together on the same wall," and "It must be a liberating feeling not to have a lot of possessions around." When Anna stepped out of the closet, the women were gathered around Merritt, perusing Anna's prints.

"Hmmmm, interesting."

"But they're so depressing -- "

"That's the intention, obviously. This is serious art, Bren!"

"I know, but I don't think I could live with so much reality on my walls."

"How do you make these?"

"It's an intaglio process; the ink comes from recessed -- "

" -- How interesting."

"Wow."

"Hmmm, yes."

They set the prints down, stood uncomfortably, hands in pockets, adjusting their scarves, gazing around the room. These same women would have been impressed -- awed -- by the home she had lived in as a lawyer's wife. Before her divorce. Right now, in their presence, she felt a dull ache for the easy companionship, understanding and appreciation of other artists. It irritated her to be made to feel this way in her own home.

"Oh, now *this* I like."

The woman with the TV stood in the bedroom doorway, looking at the painting across the room, the one Anna had done on her New Mexico honeymoon and then had ripped up during a sleep-walking episode shortly before she left her husband. The painting was her memory of sleeping in the desert, how still everything seemed, then the realization of unseen movement -- lizards, bats, wind. There she had first realized how fast the earth was moving, how many stars there were, how small she really was. And then, in the morning, her amazement at that bone-bleaching sun taking over, the fast changes in light and temperature. From the doorway, the woman couldn't see the rip in the canvas. Anna immediately regretted having left the painting out where it could be seen.

"Oh, that's just something I was experimenting with. It's quite old, not what I'm doing now."

"Oh no, I *love* this!"

The woman walked across the room, bent over the painting, saw the rip and looked back, alarmed, at Anna in the doorway.

"It -- there was an accident -- "

The woman saw Anna's dismay and came to her side. "I'm sorry. How rude of me to just walk in there."

She squeezed Anna's arm and smiled sympathetically. Anna felt a tightening in her throat. If only they would just leave. Soon they did. At the door Merritt laughed and hugged Anna. Even Merritt didn't realize her anguish, her signs of dismay. Anna felt even more aware of her aloneness, but hugged her friend extra hard.

Anna spent so much time alone these days, she rarely observed herself in contrast. When she did, she became aware that the transplanting to Chicago was not correct. She would need, soon, to relocate to wherever her roots could take hold, wherever she could find kin, whether with other artists or alone in a sympathetic environment. Some place like the New Mexico of her honeymoon, where she could feel at ease with herself and not be stumbling into encounters which made her feel inadequate and vulnerable. After letting the women out the door, she turned and tried to see her rooms through their eyes.

Not the dwelling of a mature, directed woman. Too eclectic, too much make-shift. The brick & board shelving, the mattress on the floor, the unframed prints taped to the wall -- the ones she couldn't yet decide how to frame -- the mason jars of plant cuttings, just starting to spread new shoots. No large, potted rubber trees or eight-year-old trailing philodendron, those decorator magazine suggestions of stability. The details of her apartment which usually delighted her eye -- patterns of lace and night shadows on the wall, the quilt smoothed down just so -- now seemed so shabby, embarrassingly adolescent.

She riffled through the prints they had seen. *Too depressing. Too much reality.* The words stung.

Alone. *Don't you get scared?* She walked from the living room to the bedroom to the kitchen to the bath. It seemed secure, the windows too high for easy access, the doors double-locked. It had not occurred to her, until the women's comments, to be afraid in the apartment. On the streets she was wary. The presence of campus, neighborhood and city police cars constantly patrolling, the white security phones at every corner, all served as caution of the area. But at night in her own apartment, her internal pre-occupations overwhelmed concern for her physical safety.

One weekend while visiting Merritt's, Anna had followed the TV report of the rape and murder of a young woman at an ICC station on the north side. She felt uneasy from it for days after. Had people always existed with this fear of being violated or killed at any time? How did one live with it, so nonchalantly? Anna raged at everything she couldn't do because of the fear of violence. Live the life of a potential victim. Stay home at night, don't stand near the windows, don't be seen. It was futile to rage. It was just how things were. She hated it.

All in all, a disturbing evening. Everything challenged: her lifestyle, her art, her safety. Her life alone was too new to counter the women's challenges.

She was irritated at herself for perceiving their innocent comments as an attack. Had she invited the criticism? Or had she heard comments as criticisms which were in fact simple expressions of surprise at a different way of living? It was hard not to see it as malicious; those who chose the safe paths chastised her for daring to experiment.

Before falling asleep, Anna spread the prints out on the bed and looked at them, one at a time, trying to see them as the women had. Yes, they were, at first glance, depressing. But each one pulled her in -- reexamination of details, reentry into the moment of creation -- she could not force objectivity. She stacked them carefully on the trunk next to the bed, turned out the lamp and lay back in the dark. She had trouble falling asleep; familiar noises she usually didn't even hear jerked her back to consciousness. The refrigerator, floor boards that creaked with no footsteps, the wind, street noises...

◊ ◊

...Cramping began at noon. Anna woke to alarming light, shielding her eyes with the sheets. Too many covers. Sticky sweat. Must wash these sheets, too much of Collin's scents in here, that ambivalence she felt at having let him back into her bed, despite the death of passion between them. She felt vaguely guilty about their sex these days, guilty for letting herself take a purely physical comfort with him, as if she were exposing herself to an aspect of life which would change her irreversibly. She feared she would never be able to take passionate feelings -- her own or anyone's -- seriously again, now that she knew the death of passion.

Her eyes were puffy in the vanity mirror. What was that poem she'd read once, about harsh words and awaking to innocence? One of those days. Innocent. Whatever responsibility she usually took for her life, today she was innocent. No wrong in anything she did, even ambivalent sex in her own bed. Why had she drunk so much wine with those women? Anna passed her work table on the way to the bathroom, holding her nightshirt to her crotch to stop the blood flow. Work? No, not today. Clean up, eat something, take a book and go back to bed. Lost day.

She showered in lukewarm water, then, at the end, cold, to awaken her skin. She hopped up and down as she dried herself. It was the cramping that made her feel innocent, somehow. That feeling on period days -- an aching, a vague longing. Yet it was a soft rising, a feeling of well being, of being loved. Loved? Yes, by herself. Making a child of herself. Oatmeal and PJs and back under the covers. Soft lamp light of childhood room. Parents' voices down the hall.

Collin came by as she was pouring tea. Sprawled on the floor pillows and talked aloud to himself about some woman he'd met at the lakefront last night. Why did he tell her these things? Trying to make her jealous? Or were they really such friends now that it didn't matter? It felt so funny not to care. To just hear it as a rather amazing story. Amazing to her. To him it was just streetlife, as usual. But who was this man she spent time with? This "Collin"? All the energy and intelligence to have everything society offered, but he stubbornly chose to wear the desert boots, hitch the routes, warm the bar stools.

At dusk they walked to the Polynesian restaurant on 53rd. A crisp night, the buildings and lights and their breath sharp-edged. That Maxwell Parrish purple-blue sky as the sun left. In the restaurant, amid the dark red lamps and fish net ceiling, they ordered from the American side of the menu, as people hungering for other than food. Hot buttered rums, onion rings, fried chicken dinners, maybe desserts later.

"You know, it's funny, Collin. We spend more time together and tell each other more truths than we ever would if we were lovers or married."

"We're not lovers?"

"You know what I mean -- it's just for comfort, with us. Not like passion, or -- "

Collin smiled at her in mock seduction.

"You mean not like that first time, after you'd left your husband and I was your big adventure?"

"No."

Anna frowned into her drink. Sometimes the changes were overwhelming. That first night seemed very far away.

Collin gave her his older brother smile, patted her hand. "We're just two lonely people, Anna. That's all. There's a lot of us."

Anna curled back into the corner of her booth, her feet tucked under her, taking comfort from the steam of her rum cup. It was true, what he said. Anna felt alone with him, yet as if alone next to a fireplace. Not like with a lover, not that kind of fire that you stare into and become lost in. With Collin it was more like those gas logs whose flame pattern was repetitive and you soon tired of watching, wishing it were a real fire, but still stayed for the heat. Biding time until something better, the real thing, came.

"So, have you thought more about what's next for you?"

Anna had been telling him her thoughts of leaving Chicago the last few times they met. She shrugged, sipped.

"I still think you should just pack up and go to New Mexico. I got a feeling while I hitched through there this summer, about you. That's why I brought you that tortoise shell I found by the side of the road. Route 66. Kept thinking of you, Anna."

"Nah. You were just thinking of me because I was the last woman you did it with before you hit the road."

Collin laughed, clinked his hot rum with hers. "No, that's not true."

"I wasn't the last one?"

He laughed again, not even embarrassed.

"You know me, Anna. What does that matter? I can hardly keep track, actually. No, it was *you*. I really felt something for you there. There are a lot of artists there, you know? And no wonder, that light. Time is peculiar there, too. Like, in some ways, time's stopped there about 1965... yet, in other ways, it's way ahead of us. The way people think and see things. Creative energy, in the air, in the sun. Even the cacti seem to vibrate with it. Well, you know, you were there once."

"I was. And you've made me think of it again."

"You might paint there again."

"Yes, I might."

The idea excited her more than she wanted to say as yet. She needed to think of it in secret, not to have any other influence on her decision. She had to go somewhere. Chicago was just a landing place. Most people she knew here, in the university community, would be leaving in the spring. She had made no deep connections with the natives. It would be that way, here, in Hyde Park. She would become one of the strange displaced hangers-on, and her friends would be students coming and going. She knew some Hyde Parkers who had rented the same place for decades, with roommates changing from semester to semester. That wasn't what she wanted. Nor to wait for the graduate student who would inevitably arrive with his dreams to carry her off with him to Boston or L.A. or Denver. Not that. She wanted to move alone, to make a choice for herself that had nothing to do with any man. To find a place, take the risk, and go. New Mexico had occurred to her, even before Collin brought her the tortoise shell. Those few days on her honeymoon, the ripped canvas. It pulled at her, that place.

Their dinners came and they ate in silence, filling the

hollows. Alone but together. The rum and soft red lights, the
snow outside, the bored, drooping eyes of the bartender, leaning
on his elbows. This insufficient, sad joining in this too-big city,
her menstrual cramps softening to an almost pleasant ache, her
toes warming now... it all felt good and, somehow, enough.
    A young woman was the only other patron tonight, sitting
two tables away from them. She was pretty, curling brown hair,
sherbet pink mohair sweater. She sipped slowly at a second pina
colada in a tall glass, garnished with a pink paper umbrella. Her
first one, a cloudy empty glass, sat next to it. The waiter
brought her dinner. BBQ ribs. Anna wondered idly why such
a beautiful woman was eating alone. Then wondered at the
sexism of her thought. But it was that the woman looked
vulnerable, looked dressed for a date, yet was alone. A conflict
of images. And the strange attempt at festivity with the drinks
-- the paper parasols. Not the serious scotch-on-ice or wine of
a woman alone. Anna looked back to her plate.
    "I am so lonely."
    Anna looked up quickly at the woman. She was cutting her
ribs slowly, concentrating. Had the woman really said that?
Anna had distinctly heard her. There were no other women in
the restaurant; it had to be her. But it was strange: the woman
didn't seem distressed, wasn't crying; she was just cutting her
food, looking into her plate. Had Anna imagined it? Anna
watched her, wanting to do something. Maybe she should go
ask the woman to join her and Collin. Maybe the woman was
on an edge, even suicidal. So out of control as to have said that
aloud. But it might do more harm than good to say anything to
her, to make her position obvious. And what if Anna had
imagined it? The woman would then be embarrassed or
irritated. Her position would then be acute. It was hard enough
for a woman to eat alone in a restaurant, especially at night,
especially one so festive. To have a stranger come up and
comment on it would be just too much.
    Anna looked at Collin, who was now reading a paperback
from his jacket pocket, *Fear and Loathing in Las Vegas*,

propped between the sugar bowl and the edge of his plate, as he cut his food with urgency. Dear Collin, his crazy energy, tackling two things at once with equal intensity. Something welled up in her, watching him. Crazy man. His life a mess, no direction, yet his energy to keep at it never relented. That heat that had first attracted Anna to him. She looked over at the woman. She hadn't eaten her food, was slowly pulling her arms into her jacket sleeves. Her second pina colada almost full, the paper umbrella not even removed from the rim. Anna felt a panic. What if the woman was leaving to go cry alone? Or worse? It came to her like words from outside, like the woman's voice had. *No one should be so alone.* There was no reason for this. Anna wanted to take Collin by the arm, lead him to the woman, say, "He is just my friend. Let him stay with you tonight. He will help you. Take him." Collin would be just what this woman needed; he would be perfect. He would give her body heat and stroke her into feeling valuable; he would give her some of his energy and strength, challenge her to --

But there was nothing Anna could do. The young woman walked out into the night slowly, somnambulistic.

Later, Collin walked Anna back to her apartment. She let him stay the night, in her ambivalent sheets.

◇   ◇

...Over Merritt's shoulder, Anna watched the hazy black and white torso pushing up through the tray of fixative.

"Here it comes. I thought this the best going-away present I could give you."

Jacket lapel, fingers of right hand gripping a glass, eyes staring off to the left. Oh yes, the photo Merritt had taken when Anna first arrived -- was it? --

"The first night. The night you landed on my doorstep and said you'd left your husband, remember?"

Anna remembered. There had been a dinner party going on when Anna arrived. She had sat in a corner with a full plate of leftovers, shaky from the incredibility of her move, suddenly ravenous. And a glass that Merritt kept filling with wine. She

had huddled back in a corner of the sofa and watched, listened
to the noise and movement of the party, unfamiliar voices,
academic and political discussions alien to her. *This is where
I've landed?* she thought, yet too exhausted emotionally to try to
evaluate her new surroundings. Now Anna stared down at the
photo as the features of the face sharpened. Her eyes stared to
the side, vague, a smile almost, but not. An emotion she could
not name. Fear? Confusion? A vague emotion, a reaction.

"And this one," Merritt said as she pulled another photo from
a tray of stop bath and slid it into the fix with a pair of tongs.

Anna watched herself again, evolving on paper.

"Last week, remember?"

Merritt took it in the kitchen at Anna's going-away party.
Anna was turning from the refrigerator with ice cubes in her
hand, caught off-guard by the camera. Caught in a laugh, from
the side, her eyes grabbing at the camera in passing. A
sharpness, eyes saying, "Look at me! I know what you see!"
Something alive in that face, as if she was having a joke on
anyone who would see the photo.

Changes, then. The gift of changes. Anna hugged her friend
around the waist, close, hard.

Two more stacks of posters and prints to pack and that would
do it. She would finish the overnight bag in the morning.
Remember to make coffee for the thermos, too. The curtains --
leave them. Anna pulled down another empty box from the
closet and began rolling posters and stacking frames between
towels. The Hopper's *Nighthawks* poster stopped her. Never
did decide how to frame it. She held it open a few minutes
before rolling it and wrapping it with a rubberband. That would
be important in New Mexico, to have that reminder on her wall.
The stark night corner, the man, the woman, their faces, their
shoulders hunched with as much held inside as would compensate for the emptiness of the dark, half-shaded windows in the
building behind the cafe. Everything in that picture having
anything to do with life and movement was in those two people,

in the indecipherable thoughts of the lone man to their left, in the words the cook was saying, in the woman's fingers playing with the matchbook. Where were they headed? In motion.

Anna met Collin in the Greek restaurant on 57th for baklava and coffee. Her body ached with fatigue from the day's packing, the last minute things left to do. Anna felt dull, pale, hardly aware of Collin, only vague relief that this would probably be their last meeting. Collin rolled his eyes drolly and rubbed his palms together when the sticky cakes arrived. Anna smiled at his antics which had once filled her belly with warm chills. She sipped her coffee reverently -- the caffeine would be nothing less than life tonight, the packing to finish, hair to wash. Watching him eat she felt a momentary regret that the time of warm chills was gone. With the half rueful smile that substituted for conversation she stared at the reflections of Collin, herself, the counter and coffee cups through the dark window.

"Do you believe in the poignancy of life?"

Collin looked up, stared at her, his eyes wide, his mouth set. Anna had expected him to laugh, to say something derisive. "Oh, Anna, of course. Oh, yes."

Very softly staring, his eyes clear, into hers. For a moment their eyes held, then she lowered hers to her coffee, smiling wistfully. In this light, her face was chalky, the lines of protection and aging exaggerated. Older and leaner and harder than she wanted to appear.

Collin lit a cigarette, held it between his fingers, his hand resting near hers on the counter. She leaned forward on one elbow, fingering a matchbook, staring intently into it, beyond it. White china coffee mug at her elbow. Collin's jaws clenched, his mouth grim. Against what he would say.

"Have you ever thought about us? That maybe we might get together again -- like the first time? I mean, really like lovers?"

Anna fingered the matches, kept her face still. How could he ask that? Couldn't he see she wasn't that person anymore, did not need him to play that role for her? Or were the changes only apparent to her? No, the changes were real. It was his blindness that wished not to see them. But how to answer? He had been important, an important movement in her life. She chose her words carefully.

"You can't go back."

A cliche. A generality. Nothing personal, just how it is. He chuckled. That slow chuckle, his eyes direct on her. Seeing through her, knowing her thoughts, her care. Hiding his hurt with a laugh, but a laugh with a trace of malice in it. Knowing she wasn't fooled by it. They both clutched white china cups as the waitress refilled them.

It exhausted her. Her life. These late coffee talks with men. The coming together, the splitting apart. Never meeting at the exact place, miscommunications. There had been passion between them, but long ago, in another time.

"Anyway, this doesn't sound like you. Old foot-loose?"

He grinned out the window into the night. "Oh yeah, sure. It's not me, really. Just that -- well, I've been feeling a new attraction toward you lately. Silly stuff, Anna."

"What do you mean?"

"Oh..." He was so like a boy child at this moment, shrugging, meeting her eyes with a grin, not seeing in them what he hoped for, sliding his glance away, back outside the window, the protective grin slipping momentarily. "...I guess it's really just... admiration. I admire what you're doing. Like that Dylan song, you know, 'Always have respected her for doin' what she did and gettin' free.' But I'll miss you. Guess if I thought you'd take me seriously I'd never have told you to go to New Mexico."

"I don't believe that for a moment."

He laughed, brought his gaze back in from the night window, fighting his embarrassment, to her relief; it was so disconcerting to see the emotion on his face. She had counted on him to be flippant at this goodbye, warm as a brother, but the jester. She was too exhausted from packing and directing herself toward the Southwest to think how to respond to anything unexpected at this moment.

"Naw, you're right. I do want you to go. It's right for you. Forget what I just said -- "

"I won't forget it. But I'll remember it for what it is -- just a confusion of emotions."

Collin eyed her, a comical, quizzical look on his face. "Am I confused?"

"Hey, Collin, we've been pretty close the last few months since you got back from hitching to California. Now I'm leaving. You're just at a moment in your life between trips. I mean, you're not sure what you're doing next, right?"

"I'm so transparent?"

"You're restless. So... we've been kind of a port in the storm for each other. And now the port is closing down. Maybe you're a little shaky -- but it'll be as good for you as me. Now you can get on with whatever's next. Or, knowing you," she ribbed him, "You already have." He grinned and cut into his baklava, chuckling. "Yeah, I thought so. Hell, Collin, if I weren't leaving, right now you'd probably be giving me some paranoid 'Hey, it's great being pals but I met this woman last night so don't be pissed' routine. Am I right? Am I right?"

Collin shook back his head and laughed loudly, stomping his boot under the counter.

"Ah, Anna, I'll miss you. Always know where I stand with you. Crystal clear. So, it's tomorrow morning, eh? For real?"

"For real."

For real. Anna imagined for a moment, watching him eat, that she had been watching this same man over thousands of cafe counters eating thousands of late night desserts. If it were another time, she another woman, she could have been Collin's wife, a woman who stayed despite the drinking and womanizing. They would have battled it out into some kind of compromise or unvoiced bitterness. Facing each other across the table like this, seeing each other clearly, all traces of romance gone, they might have found a way to live with that pure knowledge, the cynicism, the pale affection of it. And perhaps if they got past a period of alienation they might have fallen back together for comfort in aging, two people on a porch rocking with crickets. Perhaps we could go off and live our lives, Anna thought, and then meet again in thirty years, set up housekeeping, wait out the end, feed each other? In a simple cabin on a beach?

But time would erase that fantasy as cleanly as it had erased her passion.

She left him smoking. Passing the window outside, she noted for the first time that the smile he wore was the same removed one as her own reflected in the window. Walking through the light snow, lit by blue city lights, she knew which self she was leaving in his hands: the purely sexual being. With him she had tested her sexual power; there had been nothing between them but the urgency of sex, the handing back and forth of the power of it. Withholding, attacking, giving.

Perhaps there was nothing more real than that out there. Maybe that was why the older generations had not moved so easily into divorce, had clung despite that disappointing reality discovered in the mate. Because they knew this was all they would ever find with anyone. Crack the myth, make the same motions on the mattress enough times, it was a formula, a law of physics, unchallengeable. If that was so, then at this point, as far as she could see -- which was only as far as the road to New Mexico -- she did not want it.

Better she find out her own disappointing truths and learn to accept them, than discover them with dismay in another's eyes...

The Red Silk Kimono

A Script Without Dialogue

Time: Now
Place: A City
Characters: Business Woman
             UPS Man
             Six Living Mannikins

A very simple two-level modern apartment. Furnishings are sparse but expensive (built to last) and without imagination. No personal expressions are visible on the walls. It is difficult to detect the personality of the resident from the furnishings, unless it be a sternness, a withholding nature, one who imagines herself worthy of finer things but only as a quiet statement to herself, not to be used or shared. A glass cabinet holds fine, elegant china that is never used.

In the bedroom, somber, dark-colored clothes are hung on a series of six living mannikins standing in a row to represent a closet. (Underneath the clothes they wear identical flesh-tone leotards, a few of them are only in leotards -- as if they are empty hangers -- at the opening of the scene; their hair is pulled back unadorned so that they look as much like each other as possible, and they stand in identical positions, all facing the same direction off stage.)

It is early evening. Enter the resident, a woman in her late 30's dressed in severe conservative lines -- dark business suit, low heels, dark overcoat, gloves, leather briefcase. It is obvious that her evening movements upon entering her apartment are highly ritualized, never varying. She places the briefcase on a desk, at right angles to the desk's corners. Removes her gloves, places them neatly on top of the briefcase. Goes to the bedroom, removes her coat, drapes it on a mannikin. She moves the mannikins as if they are attached to a clothes rack, they move passively under her hands. Sits on the bed, removes her shoes, places them near the mannikins.

As she removes her suit jacket, the door buzzer sounds. Mild aggravation, instinctual response of her body -- being interrupted in the next action of hanging the jacket has thrown her -- unsure what to do, buzzer sounds again, she leaves the jacket, goes to the door, irritatedly checking her wrist watch as she does. At the door is a UPS man with a package, she signs for it, he smiles, being friendly, she is curt and ends the exchange quickly, closing the door. She shows no curiosity about the package, places it on a table, goes back to the bedroom, continues hanging the jacket on a mannikin, removes the blouse and skirt until she is down to her slip, drapes the blouse on a mannikin, folds the skirt and drapes it over the arm of the mannikin, then removes a dark, mannish bathrobe from one mannikin and puts it on. Goes back downstairs, puts on a kettle for tea, removes a covered dish from refrigerator, puts it into oven. Sits at table, opens evening paper to the business section, tries to concentrate.

Now the box has her attention, against her will. She starts to go over to it and is stopped by tea kettle whistling. Relieved for the excuse not to yet approach the box, she goes to the stove, prepares the tea, sits back down with the paper. But the box again beckons. She rises, starts to go toward it, smells her dinner, relieved again, goes to oven, removes it, sets it on the kitchen table. At table she glances over to the china cabinet for a long moment, deciding. Goes to the cabinet, touches the glass almost wistfully, puts her hand on the knob, then stops herself, her face composed again, goes back to kitchen, selects a simple, day-to-day plate from a cabinet, sets her place with folded napkin, correctly placing the utensils as if for a formal gathering. Sits to eat. Takes one forkful, her attention again drawn to the box. Forces herself to eat her meal, going against her obvious wish to open it and satisfy her curiosity.

After eating, she gives the box a stern look as if it is a child that must wait until the dishes are cleared. Clears the table, puts everything away, dishes in the sink, etc. Then turns, wiping her hands on a towel. Faces the box, goes to it. Reads the return address, a shadow of pain and rigidity quickly replaces an initial look of surprise and delight. Turns away, as if not to open the box, then turns back, opens it. There are two brightly and elaborately wrapped birthday presents inside. She opens the first one; it contains a cake box. She lifts the lid only partially, closes it, places the box in the center of the kitchen table. Opens the second package. It is an antique, elegant red, silk kimono with embroidered flowers and birds. She is stunned, sits, holding it in her lap, impressed with its value and beauty. This is the first time we have seen her lose herself a bit.

She stands, holds the kimono up to herself, starts to put it on, stops. Folds it neatly, sets it down. Gathers the wrappings and puts them in a garbage bag, puts the garbage bag in a trash can in the kitchen. Locks the door, turns out the downstairs lights, starts to go upstairs. Stops, looks at the kimono, goes back, picks it up, takes it with her upstairs.

The upstairs lighting is soft, a lamp. She places the folded kimono on the bed. Takes a nightgown from a drawer, steps out of our sight behind the mannikins, returns wearing the nightgown, drapes the bathrobe on a mannikin, picks up the kimono. For a moment we think she will put it on, but she takes it to the clothes rack, hangs it on a mannikin. It is clear that, to her, the kimono looks out of place with her somber clothes. She rearranges the clothes so that the kimono is sandwiched between darker pieces, as if to hide it. She goes to the dresser, combs her hair without looking in the dresser mirror. Sets her alarm, gets into bed, turns out the lamp, goes to sleep.

The kimono seems to glow in the dark, a soft pulsating light emanating from it. Slowly, the mannikin wearing it begins to move, almost imperceptibly -- we think it is our imagination, a trick of the light at first -- but then she is clearly moving, gracefully, sensually, delighted with herself. She goes to the mirror, admires the kimono, turns, runs her hands over the silk, luxuriating in the feeling against her skin. Takes up the woman's comb, undoes and combs her hair with pleasure.

A soft light follows her in the dark as she glides downstairs. She opens the cake box and removes an elaborately-decorated chocolate cake, digging her fingers into the icing in an unladylike manner and sucking the chocolate from her fingers. She goes to the china cabinet, takes out a candelabra, lights it, takes out several pieces of the china, cuts large hunks of the cake and sets them out on several plates, proceeds to eat the cake, moving from plate to plate. She is a child playing out a fantasy, totally enraptured with it. Finally, she is happily weary, curls up and falls asleep on the sofa.

The light gradually goes up, daylight coming, the alarm rings. The woman wakens, turns off the alarm, sits up, feet over the edge of the bed, as if hungover. She sits several minutes, then shakes her head, rises. Combs her hair again, without looking in the mirror. Dresses, makes her bed.

Goes downstairs, seems not to notice the chaos on the table, puts on the tea kettle. Turns, begins to clean up the birthday mess as if this were an ordinary scene. Washes the good china plates, puts them in the cabinet, blows out the candelabra, replaces it in the cabinet, closes the cake box, puts the box in the garbage. Goes over to the mannikin, without expression leads her back upstairs. The mannikin is docile again, just a clothes rack. The woman places the mannikin in the rack with the other clothes, starts to go back downstairs, stops. Goes back, removes the kimono, folds it carefully. Takes the kimono back downstairs. Takes tissue paper from a drawer, wraps the kimono in the paper. Opens a drawer of the china cabinet, places the kimono carefully in the drawer. Closes the drawer. Puts on her gloves, picks up her briefcase, turns off the lights, takes one last proprietary look around the apartment, exits.

Wedding Portrait

It had been frightening at first, those nights alone in the trailer. The window over her bunk faced the main entrance off the freeway to El Coyote Cojo's gas pumps. At first the screeching of brakes and sudden headlights of the semis kept Leslie awake all night. In time it all became familiar, background noise. However, there was no getting used to the occasional banging on her door at 3:00 a.m. by truckers from Utah or Tennessee looking for the former occupant; the woman had apparently been running her own boarding business, either unbeknownst to Salazar, the truck stop owner, or with his sanction. The night also held the sounds of field rodents and wild dogs rummaging through the garbage bins behind the cafe kitchen, an occasional howling wolf, the chattering of bats. Leslie's insomnia those nights had begun her habit of 4:00 a.m. tea, lighting the kerosene lamp, sitting at the trailer kitchen table, sketching. Then, as the sun appeared behind the neon sign of the red coyote in a cowboy hat leaning on a blue crutch with his leg in a cast, Leslie would put down her pencil, stretch, stumble the three steps to the bunk, burrow under the pillow, and sleep until her shift began.

Some mornings Leslie typed invoices and letters in the closet Salazar called an office. Other mornings she helped unpack shipments of straw hats, drums and beaded belts from Taiwan for the El Coyote Cojo Curio Shop. When the staff was short-handed -- it always was -- Leslie worked the shop counter or ran the cash register in the cafe, whatever was needed. El Coyote Cojo was located at a barren northwest corner thirty miles outside of Albuquerque; no one had ever lasted more than six months at Leslie's job, but, for now, it provided the solitude, isolation and time for which she had come to New Mexico. She saw her position as temporary, a means to an end, and wanted to stay emotionally removed from everyone in these surroundings, as much as possible. The pay was good -- bribery in a wasteland -- the room and board free, so her savings in the Albuquerque bank were encouraging. Soon she would be able to quit the job, move into the city. Yes, a real house would be an adjustment. It would mean a real bathroom, for one thing; no more flashlight trips to the trucker's shower room in the wee hours. She envied Silas, the old jazzman in the next trailer; when he had to go he just stepped out back of his trailer and aimed at the sagebrush.

Old Silas. She would miss him when she left. He had moved into the next door trailer about two weeks after Leslie had arrived at El Coyote Cojo. Silas did odd jobs for Salazar, off and on, just enough to pay a meager rent on a meager trailer and keep himself in canned soup and whiskey. Leslie had been leery of the old saxophone player at first, but when he seemed not to notice her as they passed to and from the shower room, she began to rely on his presence, a non-intruding human in the next trailer.

One morning Leslie awoke with a fever. She called out to the sax player as he passed her trailer on his way to the cafe, asked him to tell Salazar she wouldn't be working today. He barely looked at her as she called out the message, did not pause in his slow walk to the kitchen entrance, but nodded, made a gesture with his forefinger and thumb that he had heard her. She made teawater, fell into a heated, skin-tingling sleep before the kettle whistled. When it did, she got up, turned off the burner, fell back into the bed, too weak to dig for tea bags. The trailer felt unfamiliar at this hour. Morning sounds were vaguely threatening. Highway traffic, laughter from the kitchen a few yards away, conversations of truckers passing from their rooms to the parking lot. The aluminum walls of the trailer seemed little protection from the assaulting sounds and intense sunlight. She pulled covers and pillows over her head and slept.

Awaking, no hunger, everything hazed at the edges, but some other hunger came forth. No one there to make tea, no toast, no lemon slices on tea saucer, no chewable aspirin. Sinking back into dismayed sleep.

Awaking, a hand nudging her shoulder. The old sax player. Dark outside. She had slept through the day. Earlier in the evening she remembered waking once, at dusk, and the sound of the saxophone next door agonizing her skin. More pillows, cursing, did he have to play every goddamn night? Leslie tried sitting up, fell back. Silas gently pushed her shoulder into the pillow, left his hand there a moment, firm, *do not get up.* She watched him light the burner under the kettle, pull down a cup from the cabinet. He sliced a lemon, then looked around the kitchen, perplexed.

"Tea pot?"

She shook her head. He made a slow sign for her to wait, left, returned from his trailer with an old, dented pot. In the gaslight it looked like pewter, but up close she saw it was tarnished silver, once a small, delicate thing, now dented and darkened.

"Found this in a dump outside Toledo, believe it? Real silver."

Leslie smiled faintly, but could not speak. The energy it took to watch his preparations exhausted her. Everything was strange to her: sounds, the sensation of blankets under her hands, his presence. Who was he now? Not the old sax player.

He brought the tea pot, set it on a fruit crate next to the bunk. Tea cup, saucer with lemon, spoon. He poured it with the care of a geisha, his hands faintly trembling. Leslie forced herself to sit up to drink it. It was so good, hot and strong. Comfort in dark colors, not like the pastel comfort of her mother's solicitations during childhood illnesses. Her throat felt like she would cry at his care, and then she realized how sick she really was, how ludicrous it was, how not like herself, how not like himself to be making her tea, to be concerned. Not the daily brusqueness she had grown used to at El Coyote Cojo. It was assumed one was spiny, like the prickly pear, if one spent time here; no one was responsible for anyone else. There was no context for this exchange between them.

"Suppose you'd like me not to play for a couple days. 'Til you feel better?"

Of course. He had seen the pillows over her head when he came in. Leslie hated to ask him not to play. Perhaps the tea was a bribe? It would be naive to think he came out of kindness. He'd probably come out of loneliness, stayed to make tea to assure she wouldn't complain about his horn. The horn came first.

"Maybe if you closed your door it wouldn't be so loud?"

"I won't play 'til you're well. You sleep now." He left. A few minutes later he returned. "You got any whiskey?"

He took the bottle she pointed out, closed the trailer door behind him. The horn or the bottle, the bottle or the horn. In the gaslight she fingered the handle and spout of the Toledo tea pot. There was a circle of leaves etched, an initial, but kicked and pounded out of recognition. She hoped he would let her keep the pot. She liked it this way, was touched by its softness, its age. As she fell asleep she heard him crooning softly on his porch step.

In the morning the fever had broken. She rinsed out the tea pot and set it on the table, hoping Silas would not ask for it back, but leaving it in view for the next time he came.

◇ ◇

Most of that summer, Silas walked evenings after his bowl of soup at the cafe. He would pass Leslie's door close to sunset, walking briskly with his hands in his pockets, as if he had an appointment. One of the kitchen dogs would look up from the

evening scraps and run to follow him. The man and the dog
would come back a couple hours later, after dark. Then Silas
would play his horn.

Tonight Leslie felt restless, sat on the trailer stoop with a cup
of coffee, waiting to see whether the caffeine or the sunset would
form her evening. Silas passed her, his head down,
preoccupied. The dog joined him. Silas stopped to ruffle the
animal's neck fur, looked over at Leslie.

"Want to walk?"

He was silent and Leslie had to adjust her step to keep up
with him. She asked where they were going. He shrugged,
jerked his head -- impatiently? -- in the direction of the railroad
tracks.

"Dump back there."

They walked on in silence. She felt amazed he'd asked her
to walk with him and aware of his irritation at her talking. He
didn't quite want to be alone, yet he didn't really want company.
Not companionship. Just presence.

Silas stopped in front of a ridge in the sand. Leslie caught up
with him. He was standing in the black remains of a small fire,
pieces of glass and plastic, clumps of layered newsprint stuck
together from last night's rain. He climbed up the ridge and she
followed. There, at eye level, about a foot from the top of the
ridge, was a layer, packed between soil layers, of the remains of
another garbage fire. As if the earth had split here, and half the
history of a burning was composted. She recalled geological
photos she had once seen, diagrams showing layers of soil, each
a different color and texture, and how each gave history to a
period of time, of change. This layer of garbage was pressed
under the current layer of soil, slowly rotting, in time to be
indiscernible, only a layer of different-colored soil.

"Wedding portrait," Silas laughed, and, climbing up over the
ridge, walked on.

Leslie stared into the layer. Broken clothes hanger, pieces of
a dinner plate, newsprint, a piece of yellowed wedding veil
hanging off, moving in the evening breeze, a wet, crumpled TV

guide. Wedding portrait. This was all that was left of a
perfume commercial, or one of those family life insurance ads,
where the heads of the man and woman bend near the fireplace,
touch foreheads softly, shy woman smile, confident man smile.
Her movie was more like a foreign film, thirty years old,
black and white, on late PBS. The screen just off enough to
cover the subtitles. Two people walking through ruins, a man
and woman who had just met at the airport that morning, both
taking planes that night to different countries. Something
quicksilver between them, because of their anonymity; the rest
only dust the woman brushed from her skirt as they stood,
staring at stones in the sun.

The scrap of wedding veil lifted in the breeze. Beyond the
ridge, Leslie could see Silas stopping over the remains of a fire,
the dog running zigzag on a scent. She crammed her hands into
her pockets and walked apart from him. Something caught her
eye -- she pulled it from the ashes. A talisman, perhaps. A
rusted cast-iron leaf, probably from a gate. She walked back to
Silas, nudged him with her elbow, handed him the iron leaf. He
turned it over and over in his palm, grunted softly, tucked it into
his pocket and went back to his rummaging.

Leslie began to search in earnest, encouraged by her find of
the rusted leaf. The field was miles of trash-fire remains; each
black circle of ash and shards might hold one real treasure.
Pocketing objects, carrying them for a while, discarding them,
altering the histories. The mildewed 1956 *Family Circle* magazine was moved to a more recent fire where broken blue plastic
astronauts lay, tiny arms poking up from matted newsprint.

Leslie remembered such days spent in her childhood, off
alone in a field, absorbed by what was under her feet, by how
it got there, by what she could pretend it was. A serenity came
over her, warming her against the evening chill. She noticed she
was smiling as she moved among the circles of ash. Silas was
yards behind, following her path, pocketing his own treasures
from piles she had already picked over. She fingered the objects
she had kept. What did her choices reveal? Part of a china

ruffle from a figurine of a dancer, a piece of melted green glass, the handle of a cup. And, from what she had not chosen, what relics was Silas collecting? She remembered the Toledo tea pot -- which he had retrieved the day after her fever -- and began to understand his absorption with the mystery of broken remnants. This ritual was a symbolic search, perhaps a kind of survival instinct after shattered lives.

Leslie watched Silas bending, fingering a plastic heel from a woman's pump. His hair was disheveled, his jacket cuff torn, his old boots caked with adobe mud in the cracks across the toe. Thin white laugh lines imbedded in the tough sun-browned cheeks. Affection welled within her.

They met, without words, sat on a small hill, waiting out the sunset. Leslie spread her treasures on the ground in a configuration, drew a circle around them with a stick, arranged leaves and pebbles in designs between them. Silas looked on with interest. He added a rusted latch part from his pocket. When they stood to leave, he superstitiously brushed away the pattern carefully with the toe of his boot. They walked back to the El Coyote Cojo, the dog circling their path, along the edge of the railroad track. Smiling faintly, their pulses high with the cool evening, the walk, the healing rhythm of their hours in the field.

Back in her trailer, Leslie lit the gas lamp and emptied her pockets, lining her treasures along the window sill. She picked up last night's sketch to work on, then put it down. Somehow it felt unnecessary to finish it, as if it were resolved. The layer of artifacts Silas had found kept returning to her in full color, black, rust, dirty white. The textures of newsprint layers, cracked china edges, the rusted pipe bent like a knee. Pale blue, browned edges of the yellowed veil. The fragility of that crinoline skeletal veil dancing against the solid earth layer.

Leslie now found herself filling a jar with water, pulling out a tablet and squeezing tubes from an old water color set she had been carrying around since school. She dipped a wet brush into a slur of hot red, moved it to mix with violet.

The sax began as she worked. Silas was composing next

door. Long, low notes like a distant fog horn, then fast dancing notes, as if the sound was trying to lift itself, then faltering back into the mournful lows. The veil in the breeze, same movement. A melody grew from that opening, first slow, a minor key. He repeated the melody, faster each time, until it became light.

Leslie's hand moved in synchrony with his music. What was the color of that refrain? A dark blue-brown, with edges heightened in a chalky green...

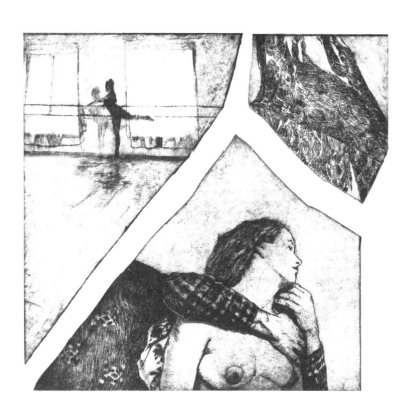

Bonsai

Experts in bonsai advise against the dwarfing of trees which produce very large leaves and/or flowers, as the effect is likely to be grotesque. These are better left alone.

single tree, leaning

Clutching his forehead and belly, Bullet lay on the thin prison mattress and laughed softly to himself, wiggling his legs, stretching the toes to the cramping point, then released. It felt just like being drunk. In order to get this high, Bullet hadn't eaten for three days. He went in with the others to meals, but just pushed the prison fare around on his plate and grinned his malevolent grin at the guards.

Yeah, it verged out-of-body, this high. Real on-the-ceiling stuff. To be specific, it was like a bottle of Jack, the sixth fast swig, plus one of those hash joints, the stuff from '73, like he used to get at Duke's farm up near Greenbay. Yeah, old Duke with the mean cur and that one-eyed Doberman. Fine, well-guarded crop, '73. Bullet laughed, slapped the bed, rolled his eyes, chuckled again. No, it had taken more than three days of not eating to get this buzz; more like thirty-seven years. He had moved through every single event of his thirty-seven years, to

get here. He could see it all connected, a logic. If the details
of his life were a mess, like lying on this itchy mattress in this
urine-smelling institution with green concrete walls, at least there
was a beauty to the logic of how he got here. He laughed again,
slapping the sheets.

A fist pounded on the other side of the wall next to Bullet's
bed. *Quiet!*

Fuck those guys. They could sleep all day through crap
games, TV, fights, lights. But at night the slightest cough --
Bullet pounded back. *Fuck you!*

He tried it again, the drunk feeling, closed his eyes,
pressing his eyeballs against the lids to induce the dizziness. It
came easier. Reached for Lenore's latest letter, pressed it to his
belly, reciting it in the dark from memory, his lips moving
Laughed again. Lenore always used to ask him what was he
saying to himself when he moved his lips like that.

"You do it all the time," she said, running her forefinger
over his lower lip. It was one of those mornings she called in
sick and he'd met her at her apartment to share his new stash.
"While driving, while eating, while walking. Only time you
don't whisper to yourself, laugh to yourself, is when we're
making love. So what're you saying?"

"Would you rather know what I'm sayin' or would you
rather do it?" He'd pushed her down into the pillows, twisting
her long, tangled black hair around his fist, and she didn't ask
any more questions the rest of the morning. He laughed now,
remembering how he could divert her curiosity simply by putting
his hand on her. She had been so responsive in the beginning,
better than any of the hippie women he'd had in the communes.
It was all new to her and he taught her what he'd learned from
them. She was one of those women who never would have
looked at him twice when he was an engineer with Hadley &
Olsen, living in a Milwaukee suburb. Women like her --
serious, scared women -- wanted something more exciting like
avant-garde poets and gunrunners to challenge their fear. Now
he had that kind of woman, and she saw him dressed in his new

mythology, the way he wanted to be seen, as if he had always been this man.

He pulled her into streetlife, was impatient with her fears. She wouldn't let go of her straight job. She wouldn't let him put stolen unemployment checks through her checking account, or let him deal from her apartment. She wouldn't do LSD. But he understood; only two years before, he too had been in the straight world. Hadley & Olsen Engineering Firm. His father and grandfather had been only foundrymen, so Bullet -- then known as Hank -- had been proud to earn the degree, the mortgage, the company softball team and Sunday barbecues, and, finally, his personal treat, the Mercedes.

The day after the car arrived, burgundy with custom black pigskin interior, Bullet drove it into the Hadley & Olsen parking lot and parked it directly under the window of Hadley's private suite. Bullet -- Hank -- strolled into the office, winking at the receptionist who had seen him drive up. She pursed her red glossed lips, squinted her false eyelashes and shook her long red fingernails, whispering, "Whoo! Hot!" Hank laughed, hitched up his slacks and loosened his H&O logo tie. By ten a.m. his supervisor had him behind closed doors advising him that neither D.W. Hadley nor Hans J. Olsen drove a Mercedes, they drove BMWs, did he get the picture? Hank shrugged. The supervisor sighed and rubbed his eyes. Hank would have to trade in the Mercedes, he explained. Maybe he should consider a Saab or even a VW bug, more in keeping with his status in the firm, did he understand?

That night Hank went home and sat in the living room with a bottle of Wild Turkey and drank it down methodically, shot glass by shot glass, whispering to himself, leaving the lamps off as dark descended. His wife lingered, worried and afraid to speak, in the hallway. But then she did speak and there was the fight, the shouting, the broken bottle, little Carla waking, screaming from a nightmare. Hank left the house, drove down by the lake, smashed up the Mercedes and stumbled home, bleeding and laughing like a mad man. The next day he told

Hadley & Olsen to go fuck each other, and, after two solid weeks of drinking, left his wife and child. He passed himself off as a journeyman molder at a small Milwaukee foundry and moved into a communal apartment near the university on the east side, where a woman gave him his first drag off a joint, embroidered snakes on his jeans and did things in bed his wife had refused to do. He only lasted three weeks at the commune; the smell of his hamburgers cooking nauseated the vegetarians, and one morning the snake woman's old man found Bullet doing her in the shower.

But there were many communes, many joints, and many women in the Brady Street head shops who were good at embroidery and hot for it. It was the 1970s and Milwaukee had just discovered the '60s and Bullet -- so named by a Viet Nam vet who sold him his first lid -- had just discovered Mao, Fat Freddy's Cat comics, Joplin and freelove. The drug community loved Bullet, with his fearlessness to rage in the streets against the system, his cool demeanor with the cops in the park. He was older than they, he'd been on "the other side." He even used to tell them not to trust anyone over 30, and he was himself 32! He became their hatchetman. The health food element and women's faction had mixed feelings when he sat in the midst of their rooms of macrame and philodendron, stabbing his cigarettes into their India brass incense burners and raucously telling The Saga of Hadley & Olsen and the Red Mercedes. He was a wild man, he drank too much and sucked their joints like candy, but he was their spokesman, their archetype. He was the King of Brady Street.

Much of the relationship between Bullet and Lenore had been wordless at first, back in 1972, when she was still so excited by him. He would call her from the corner pay phone and say he was coming over. When he got there, she'd open the door, pull him in by his bronze marijuana leaf belt buckle, and they would go at it right there in the hallway, their lips and crotches tearing at each other like small, mad animals.

Then there was the poetry. The first day they got together

she'd come up to him at the Yellow Submarine Cafe and handed him a poem about how he reminded her of some painting she'd seen at the museum, a lion on a cliff, staring into a hot fireball of a sun. Something about the lion wanting to be the sun, that it was the only thing that could compel the lion's complete respect and attention. Bullet had just had his chart done by a woman who painted a lion on his chest and explained all about his being a Leo, so he'd liked the poem, it made him hot.

They'd all been poets then, the street people. Maybe it wasn't poetry so much as an excuse to shout in public about revolution and sex, to shock the straights, and pull together with their own kind. In the bars Bullet used to get drunk and strip and read his poetry in the nude and get thrown out, screaming, "Fuckin' fascists!"

Later Lenore and Bullet added letters to their communication, while Bullet was on the road picking oranges. His were elaborate tales of the road, paraphrasings of *Leaves of Grass,* which he carried with him and propped open as he wrote on a rough wooden trailer table by a Coleman lantern. Hers were internal musings on their sex, written in her apartment under her quilts by candlelight. With her words she helped him feel connected with the parts of himself that were constantly at war, battling it out in the whisperings -- the unresolved and battered child, the male animal, the maverick, the survivor.

"Everything bursts out of you -- your heat, your anger, even the words that bubble out of you all the time in whispers," she wrote to him then. "You're not like the other men I've known. Their skin is white with the strain of holding back what they really want to do and say and be. Their eyes are tight with wrinkles of fear and their jaws are clenched against everything."

When Bullet came back to the city in between fruitpicking gigs, Lenore walked proudly next to him at the Brady Street Crafts Festival, like a queen in his world. On her sun-warmed arms were metal bracelets from the head shop, and her dark hair was braided like an Indian's with beads and feathers. Her breasts showed through the creamy gauze gypsy blouse he had bought for her and, leaning against Bullet, she let her eyes meet the sullen gaze of his male friends. He had seen how demurely she dressed for her secretarial job, when she knew she would be on the streets alone, in her bra and polyester pastel dresses with low heels, her hair pulled back, the tiny pearls in her earlobes. Afraid to shine unless under his protection, and, in his presence, compelled to flaunt herself in the shadow of his audacity. Bullet strolled in his red beret and long, redgold beard, his patchwork vest showing off his blond-haired torso, his soft embroidered jeans. The dealers, leathercraftsmen and potters called out to him, knowing he would spend his picking money at their stalls. Lenore loved being the one on his arm when the musk-scented women in flowing cotton came up to him. (Although later she would rage to him about their New Age "We're-all-open-about-this" smiles, the way they would embrace Bullet, whispering to him with their faces as close to his as lovers, as if she wasn't there.) As the women glided past, their fingers grazing his arm, they would smile at her again, and call back to her, inviting her to their bookstores, tofu potlucks, their consciousness-raising meetings, their yoga groups. Bullet was the King of Brady Street in his clothes that mocked the straights. Lenore was his apprentice, and he pulled her in, away from her straight life, her fear, her goodness.

Bullet also taught Lenore to fight, and she took to it. As it had been with all his women, the fighting was about the other women, the booze, the drugs, the violence, the dealing. Lenore feared anger. The first time he shouted at her she crumpled, and when he left the apartment to go cool off at the corner bar, she waited for him, tense with fear that he would never come back. He left another woman's apartment at 2:00 a.m. and came home, found Lenore awake and curled into a rigid embryo in the dark bed. He dropped his jeans and crawled in behind her. Her back was tense and stiff against him.

"Ah, Muffin, it don't mean nothing. Don't take it so hard," he pulled her to him.

"Why do you have to go to them?" she cried. "Why isn't it enough, just us?"

"That's just how it is with a wild man, Muffin. I won't change for any woman. I did that trip with my wife. I'm free and I won't be owned."

All these things she wrote now, all she couldn't say to him before. Now that he was locked up, now that he couldn't get angry at her. Or, he could get angry, but he couldn't do anything about it. Bang his head on these walls, maybe. It was different from being outside where he could hit some guy in a bar or shove Lenore out of the car. Here, there were no real consequences to anger. Sure, maybe a block fight, someone might even get killed, but there was nothing to explain or apologize for. Here, no one really gave a damn who got hurt.

Not that he was angry. It amused him, what she wrote. She was perfectly justified, he even enjoyed her anger. It was cool anger, she sounded so removed. Just clearing the record, no emotion. After all, it had been a few years since he'd seen her. She had a whole new life in Chicago. Bullet laughed again. *Fuck you!* If only he'd known, on the outside, about this laughing, how it could feel just as good as hitting. Might have saved him a lot of trouble. He wiggled his legs, grinning into the dark.

"You're just like a kid," she used to say. "When you're eating cake you wiggle your legs under the table. And when you're stoned. And after we've made love."

She used to tell him to himself, she saw the pouting eight-year-old bully he carried inside him, something he hadn't wanted to be, had been forced into to survive. She had funny ideas, like when she told him that men's breasts, under the right circumstances, could make milk. He laughed when she said stuff like that, but he liked her telling him; he needed the talking with her. He told her things he never told anyone else, about his old man. How when Bullet was a toddler his old man kicked him into a corner one night just because he cried. He kicked him and kicked him, until Bullet just lay there, limp, and stopped crying. And how Bullet never let himself cry again, no matter what his old man did. About how, when Carla was five years old, he himself came home drunk one night and took her squealing puppies and slammed them against the refrigerator and broke their necks, while Carla watched. Later he went into Carla's room and found her there, her father's daughter, her blond hair in electric waves, her blue, heavy lidded eyes not crying, sitting on the edge of her bed white and shaking, her hands wadded together like crumpled tissues.

"See? Even people who love you can hurt you," he'd whispered, his voice hoarse with booze and cigarettes and shouting. "Don't you ever forget that, little girl, and that it was your own daddy taught you that."

Her eyes had stared through him without seeing him.

Lenore cried when he told her these things. No one else saw the damaged and raging child in him. He'd always been the bully and now they all came to him to fight their fights for them because he was a large and strong man, physically. His dealer friends, even, would wake him in the middle of the night to go with them to collect when someone hadn't paid for his stash. A lot of late night collection calls. Sometimes coming away with money. Most times coming away with bloody fists and ransom -- stereos, antique furniture, guns, even a guy's car once. They all loved Bullet's body -- the women told him he was a stud, the smaller men saw him as a big brother, the larger ones always wanted to fight him, to prove their own bodies against his. But Lenore pushed at something else in him.

...I found the list in a folder of poems you left once. Undoing yourself constantly. I never told you I saw the list, but I never forgot it. It was names of women, in three columns. There were -- I counted -- ninety-nine names. Thirty-three in each column. I recognized some of them toward the end, before and after my name. The last name on the list was your own.

Lenore knew how things were. In her last letter she'd even

admitted she was letting herself write to him all these truths
about their time together because now he was like a caged, rabid
animal. He couldn't hurt her now and she could poke at him
through the bars -- jab, even -- and she felt a little guilty, but
jabbed anyway.

When the police picked him up six weeks ago, he'd made
the decision in the police car to just let it happen. After running
from child support for seven years, ranting in every bar between
here and Florida to anyone who'd listen. And everyone listened
after midnight in a fruit-pickers' bar. Men, women, didn't
matter. It's just *wrong,* it's *fucked,* the system *stinks,* they'd
slam their beers down with his. I mean, if a man can't make but
$200 a week, how can they make him pay $100 a week in child
support? Just because he'd been making enough during his
marriage, back when he was sitting on his ass in a hot-shot
office.

Bullet had tried that argument once, but the judge said he
was obligated to take a job that would pay as much as he had
been earning when he and his wife had the child. In order to
keep his family in the manner to which it had become
accustomed. Didn't like Bullet's explanation that he'd dropped
out into an alternative, moral life style and didn't want to
contribute $100 a week to his ex-wife's value system built on
greed and what the damn neighbor women thought. Didn't like
Bullet saying that if Goodwill was good enough for him it was
good enough for his daughter Carla. Or that she ate too much
bologna and not enough homemade bread. Contempt of court,
that time. Lenore bailed him out and he hit the road to pick
oranges. Left a lot of things, places, people. Other women.
But, inside, he never really left Lenore. Even after all these
years, what was it, four, five?

Because she knew how things were.

They got him when he ran a red light leaving town after
dropping Carla off a block from her mother's. Was it in the
police car he decided not to fight it, not get a lawyer, just go to
court, plead guilty, let them put him in debtor's prison? Maybe

he decided it earlier, maybe he ran the red on purpose. Give his ex a thrill, that was about all she'd ever get out of him. He'd had his last summer with Carla, she was getting too old to travel with him now. What was it that Lenore had said? That stuff about how she bet he would stop taking Carla summers once she was emancipated, because the only reason he did it was for the thrill of running from possible kidnapping charges. Had to take some of what Lenore said with a grain of salt, she'd as much as admitted she was jealous of how he felt about his daughter. And anyway, his ex would never bring up kidnapping. Bullet knew how Carla worshipped him, how she lived for his pay phone calls to lift her out of suburbia, his packages in the mail of underground comics and psychedelic posters, the Sunday visitations spent sitting in the dark coconut-incensed rooms with his buddies, listening to Fireside Theater. His ex knew if she had him rounded up, Carla would leave home and never come back. More importantly, she knew Bullet would never give her another cent if she had him thrown in jail for kidnapping. Anyway, before they ever led Bullet down the police station hallway, he removed himself from the whole thing, thinking ahead that now he'd have time to look at it all. Just watch it like a movie. Figure it all out, where he was headed, take stock. Thirty-seven was good for that.

...first time I ever saw you, first impression. I never told you this: in the cafe I thought you were in a wheelchair, thought the woman with you was your nurse or companion. Then to my astonishment you got up and walked out, that rolling, sexy walk. Looking at you as you moved past my table, I wondered what had caused my misperception, and decided it was because your torso was so built up and your eyes were that hot, compelling blue. I could even see the blood under your skin, that glow, like it would scald. The way you stared directly at me, sitting there with your nurse. I had figured all that power was a way of overcompensating for your lameness. Things do often hit me as direct metaphor, in the physical realm. As if what we say and do is one language that translates into a second language, only I THINK in the second language and don't have to translate. As we spent time together,

I began to understand my vision had been a premonition.

Bullet sat on the edge of the bed for an hour, staring at that letter the day it came. Then stared into the veins of cracks in the concrete floor, like dried, caked earth, or the shadows of bare tree branches on a sidewalk. His legs sucked into the plastic jail slippers like tree roots pressing vainly down. What kind of a way was that to bring a thing up? And then drop it? What about the lion poem she'd written that same night, so what was that about? A "premonition" that he was a cripple? What did that mean, anyway? Why couldn't she just say it right out?

Because of the time you'd been drinking for two days and I asked you where you'd spent my rent money and you got mad and shoved me out the car door into traffic.

Because of the time my friend was staying over and you fucked me, making more noise than usual, saying over and over, 'I love YOU,' like you had to convince us both, and I passed out and you went to the bathroom. I woke up and you were still gone so I got up to find you to come back and sleep with me, feeling all soft from our loving, and found you standing naked with an erection over my friend's bed in the dark looking down at her body.

Because of the time you called from Miami and said you weren't coming back home and had taken up with another woman and I cried and asked you to explain and you said you had to go butcher a hog and hung up.

Because of all those things I suppressed to stay with you. Van Gogh prints. Ravel's Concerto in G. Ballet lessons. Living in safe neighborhoods. Jealousy.

single tree, upright

Lenore peels the mauve, talc-stained leotard to a wad, tosses it into the tub and runs the shower steamy. Steps in, wets the leotard, rubs soap into the crotch and armpits, rinses it, hangs it over the shower curtain. Ducks her hair under the water, rubs shampoo into her hands. Itchy heat of ballet class, relieving ice of the six-block walk through Hyde Park from the Illinois

Central platform to her brownstone. Into the steam-heat apartment, sipping cold apple juice from the refrigerator. Into the hot shower. Running her body through thermal extremes. Then the flannel nightgown from the London catalogue, her familiar self-smell in it. Under the comforter on the iron bed, her cat approaching the pillow tentatively, a glass of room-temperature brandy melting one ice cube.

Tonight her ballet teacher caught her in a half-hearted leap-turn. Came to her, turning her knee out, pushing her ankle down, and said, "Try that again. Don't let your fear of falling hold your limbs back from stretching to their full capacity."

When Lenore's second try was no better than her first, he shrugged and moved on to help another dancer. His words had come at her as metaphor, without translation. She had fumbled through the leap-turn quickly and awkwardly, to run back to the dressing room and write down what he had said. Body rituals were purely language. Conversations were messages. Other conversations came to her, like the friend who had said, "Bullet goes through life in combat boots; you go through life in ballet slippers." She had laughed, had liked the image. It was true; Bullet had walked ahead through the weeds, beating back the rattlesnakes. She had followed behind in soft shoes, concentrating on the sensation of weeds against her ankles and rocks under her toes, deferring to him the survival tactics.

She thought of that first day she saw Bullet at the Yellow Submarine. A kind of man she would never have looked at before, but on this particular day, although she did not yet know it, she was ready for him, open for him.

Later she realized the openness her response to the strange man had implied. She had had enough. Of parents, of her quick and cruel marriage to a man who still had to discover he was gay. Of being shocked at those around her with their gauze clothing, bralessness, their rolled cigarettes, their feathers and beads. She wanted to *be* them, now, to know what they knew. She saw where she was headed, that eternal search for the cold, withholding father. The one who was never there, who spent his days out there, and withheld from her his secret knowledge, the only thing that could save her from her mother's fear of life, of the unknown.

At first Lenore had sought men who, like herself, were soft and fearful. No longer. She had learned that kind would hurt her with their passivity, their inability to really touch her. Not that, she said, not that gentle kind, that quiet kind, that *afraid* kind. No, she would have a man with feelings, with emotions, with anger and laughter. Somewhere she had read that to not live the height and depth of emotion was to not live at all. In one more destructive, this might have been the point at which a bottle of pills or a razor was tried, anything to cut past the surgical tapes her parents and society had wrapped around her, the softness they had put between her and reality. Reality was connected to the longing, and the longing was urgent, grew more urgent than her passivity. It was passion she longed for, the street people, poverty, blood, the noise, concrete, anger, the wild laughing.

She saw him, Bullet, who carried all of it under his skin, whose nostrils flared, whose lips were full in a sensuous pout, a slight curling of the upper lip. It was simply this: he was the first man in her life who had ever held eyes with her across a room. Audaciously, unrelentingly, probing and challenging. She did not let her eyes drop. Later he told her that was why he approached her, because she did not let her eyes drop. Of course he remembered it that way, that he approached her. But it had been that she approached him. Came to the same cafe the next afternoon and, her heart pounding, walked up to his table where he sat alone, without the woman she had mistaken for his nurse the day before. She handed him the words she had written. Not about the lameness she had seen, but about the lion. She started to move away after handing him the paper, but, as he opened it, he reached out and grabbed the fabric of her shirt sleeve and pulled her down next to him. She sat, her blood racing, a half smile on her face, staring at her hands held in a praying position on the table. He read the words, folded them, chuckled and turned to her. He put his hand on her chin, turned her face to his and kissed her hard, smashing their front teeth together, pushing with his tongue. Years later he would tell her he'd known immediately that she would not be just a one night stand. By then she would know enough of him to know he had seen her as that, exactly, an easy fuck at the Yellow Submarine.

First sex with him had been quick and rough, not what she had fantasized. She had never seen a cock so thick, so blunt. Nor had she seen one uncircumcised, which fascinated her, and was further proof to her fantasy that she had landed herself a real one, one untouched, unwounded, a raw, undamaged, fearless male. But before she had time to pull the foreskin back, he put his own hand on it, wet her with his saliva and knelt over her, pushing it into her on the shag carpet of her bare highrise apartment. Their cries were loud, hers in pain. After, she found herself bleeding. In the bathroom mirror she stared at herself, every cell in her body tingling. "He has brought me to life," she whispered to her reflection. "He has taken my virginity." Even her husband -- with all his year and a half of pushing into her, his conviction that she was frigid, her fear it might be so, his hard-voiced urgings to her to *come* -- had not succeeded in breaking her, in bleeding her. But this man had, this man with no fear, this Bullet, who did what must be done, as a natural course.

She went back to bed and he held her, smiling, purring like a large cat. "I'm sorry it was so fast, I always go fast at first." But she was opened, her vagina burning and pulsing, and she was glad of it. His fingers moved down and began to touch her as she had never been touched. The heavy lids of his eyes, the fullness of his lips, fuller now than they had been in the cafe, pulled at her and made her moan.

So they began their lovemaking, which was always fierce. Of course, once she realized she was not the only one he gave his body to, that there was no woman he could give more than his body to, other things began to happen. Where she used to be wet before he walked in the door, he began to use jelly and saliva. Where her nipples had been sensitive to his mere proximity, now they were numb. When they hardened to his fingers, she stared down at them in amazement, for she couldn't feel them at all, as if they weren't part of her body. Her body began to protect itself from him, to not trust itself to be so vulnerable to him. A woman friend said, "You let him hurt you too much." Another said, "By being with that kind of man you expose yourself to his karma." Years later Lenore realized the reason for their warnings -- that he had gone to their doors at night behind her back. Distanced by time, she wondered if they had let him in. But of course they had. When they had asked why she was with such a brutal man, she had told them he was a paper tiger, a big, gentle cat. She had told them how he was, his size, his raw loving. She had been such a child, so trusting. The night he came home with a small braid woven into his hair, the kind her friend Rainbow was doing with her own hair those days, Lenore had not suspected.

She protected herself, hardened herself to him in some ways, but did not, would not, could not leave. She had been bound too long, been tied so tight that her limbs had not yet recovered their blood flow. He was fire, dangerous flame, and her hands were still cold, still waking up. She warmed herself on him, and when he singed her with his anger and drinking and womanizing, she cried out and hit him and shouted. Then they touched and kissed and moaned. That soft moaning in twilight, half clothed, urgent, no time for undressing. The ripping of fabric, pulling back of skin and entering, the feeding where they had, as children, been told not to touch. He was soft, under his clothes. Vulnerable, in his nakedness. His buttocks white and dancing, his scarred shoulder which sat lower than the other, his feet and hands large like cat's paws. He was her animal, in his wildness and his need. For this, in delight, in defiance, she stayed.

But, always, after, they lay, not speaking, each staring at the billowing window curtains. Until he rose silently, dressed and left. Came home hours later, smelling of beer, his hardened facade back, his smile malevolent, challenging her not to ask, not to speak, not to care.

◇ ◇

Lenore sat on the dressing room bench, inhaling her sweat, staring down at the words of her ballet teacher on her lap, thinking of Bullet. Of how he was to her an archetype, the embodiment of all that the male animal could be and yet was so wounded, so warped against being. Parents, society, the expectations to be strong and silent. The women, like her, who came to touch him with compassion and left with their fingernails sharpened. The war, the times, the life.

Another conversation -- the writer she had met on Amtrak, the summer she left Bullet, the one who spoke an unfamiliar yet intriguing language, referred to books and music she'd never heard of. In a few hours the man made her acutely aware of the life of the mind she had neglected while in Bullet's company. As they sat side by side in the train's night motion, sipping coffee from styrofoam cups, the man had asked, "Have you ever known yourself to envy a man his strength, to align yourself with a man who was not afraid of the things you were afraid of? Only to, like Delilah, stick in the knife in the night, cut off the hair? And called that love?" The question had disturbed her. She didn't know what it was in her face, she a stranger, that would cause another stranger to ask such a question.

Conversations were messages.

Like the one yesterday with the Green Assassin. She'd run three blocks to catch her train and was coughing from the cold air and exertion as she climbed the steps to the ICC platform.

"How long you had that cold?"

A pale, sweaty man with stiff shoulders stepped forward in a lime sherbet tuxedo jacket, ruffled green tux shirt, kelly green and yellow polyester plaid slacks, and dark ski goggles. His hair was greased back, his shoes polished white over black. His forehead was red, peeling, blistered.

"Oh, just got it."

"Yeah, me too. Last one I got was when they tried to kill Reagan. Had it three weeks. Got one when Kennedy went, too. And once those people in that car over there in front of that restaurant, they gave me a cold."

Lenore looked where he pointed with his red finger. A man and two women were getting out of a silver LTD. The man was black, in a long caramel leather coat, the women Hispanic with long, wavy dark hair, one in jeans and a purple fur jacket, the other in a bronze jumpsuit and disco heels. The woman in the heels slipped on the ice, laughing, and grabbed the arms of the other two for balance.

"They kidnapped me from that parking lot and made me go with them. They tortured me, stuck pins under my nails."

The Green Assassin spread his hands. The fingers were swollen and red.

"And then they dumped me back in that parking lot the next morning. I can't tell you all the things they did to me, you a nice lady. It's the women shooting the presidents and popes, because women can't shoot for shit. They always miss. They don't aim to kill. They aim to injure. It's cruel; they do it to torture a person. I know about killing. I was in the army. I know how to handle a gun. It's those assassinations that give me a cold. I would shoot to kill, none of that."

Lenore stared into the parking lot until the ICC came, half turned away from, half toward the Assassin, so he wouldn't think she wasn't listening and get angry. She held her breath and tightened her knees. Clenched her fists in her pockets and discovered Bullet's latest letter in one of them. Strange letters, so controlled, such sparse, distanced descriptions, as if he weren't involved.

From the rulebook:
14. Disruptive conduct & prohibited acts
Section .1 killing
.4 rioting
.6 taking hostages
.8 escaping

.32 insolence toward a staff
member
.49 shouting, singing & whistling
Above bed is a 'Push for Help' button.
Dinner entrees are:

Sun	*chicken*
Mon	*beef*
Tues	*hot dogs*
Wed	*pork*
Thur	*fish*
Fri	*ring bologna*
Sat	*corned beef*

This way you know what day it is. On TV they let us watch cartoons and sports, no news. (Are we at war?) I'm caught up in an urgent matter, interior investigation. I'll leave with a clean slate, a body and mind in prime condition. The rest must be done meticulously and with my whole heart. All this sitting around causes epidemics of hemorrhoids. I do 200 situps a day on the bed. Otherwise, I sit as little as possible, play checkers standing up. That way, I'll get varicose veins instead of hemorrhoids. People aren't built for inactivity.

She wasn't sure why she was allowing this renewed correspondence with Bullet. Hadn't heard from him in three years, not since his last surprise visit to her brownstone apartment. With his head shaved and sniffing glue and picking up women in the ICC station bar downtown and telling her the details later. Lenore had no feeling for him at that point, except a curiosity and a disconcerting emptiness at not desiring him after all their years of passion. She even had sex with him one night, to find out what that would now be. It was exciting, like a pornographic movie, familiar yet strange. But with no emotion. She let him stay a week, hoping if he was around a bit she'd begin to recognize what it was about him she had loved so much before, or what it was she had thought he could teach her. But he frightened her neighbors, ridiculed her music and books, yelled drunkenly up to her window from the street about her "rarified atmosphere" and alienated the few friends she had made. So she told him to leave. He had smiled, coolly, quickly gathered up his backpack of belongings, bowed to her and left. Holding onto some mad dignity only he understood. There was no dignity left between them. He was what was left of the street life of their '70s. Now a skeleton, a ghost. Embarrassing, like an old dashiki in the bottom of a drawer, an old hash pipe shaped like Pan. His view of the world no longer applied. The street drugs were now weakened or, worse, tainted and laced with poisons. The street people were madmen, conmen and addicts. There was no more India gauze, no more feathers, no joy. There was no love. Lenore herself, at the time he had arrived, was recovering from an affair with a gaunt, married, guilt-ridden history professor who had introduced her to Gibbons, Ptolemy and Remy Martin cognac. With his white skin and fear-wrinkled eyes and clenched jaw. In this context, Bullet was an aggravation, an embarrassment.

Now these letters between them. That old curiosity, still, that was stronger in her than the desire to deny the existence of the Bullets and Green Assassins of the world. The protections she devised to isolate herself from street life scared her more than street life scared her. It made her feel vulnerable to no longer have dealings with the alien culture, as if the street people knew something she also needed to know, for survival. Something ballet couldn't teach her.

Lenore sighed, stuffed the scribblings into her gym bag and returned to class to try the leap turn again.

tree with high, exposed roots

In the morning, Bullet couldn't move his legs. He woke suddenly, sweating, crying out, sitting up quickly. Except there was a weight on him and he couldn't sit up. He heaved forward with his chest and propped up on his elbows, but his legs wouldn't move. A piece of his dream -- what had it been? -- something rough -- a texture -- burlap? -- wrapped around him -- sucking -- a woman's breast -- her scent -- Lenore's, that scent she used to --

He called out. The others stared in at him; the guards came and carried him to the infirmary, hanging his arms over their shoulders, dragging his legs. He didn't feel the sides of his feet scraping on the concrete.

After the doctor examined him -- Bullet watched his reflex reactions, but could not feel them -- the shrink came. This was OK, Bullet thought. He had some things to get to the bottom of. Maybe this guy would have some answers. Bullet stared up into the ceiling light.

"I know you what you want me to talk about. It's that sensation that comes to me before sleep sometimes. Often. We could talk for months about my mother and my marriage and my kid and all that, but I know that that sensation is the root of it, where we'd have to end up. So we can just start there. I can tell you, though, it's no use. I've tried to name it, you see, I know, I *know,* if I could name that sensation -- it's like a piece of a dream you almost remember and then you're awake and it's lost. If I could name it, all of this would end."

"All of what?"

Bullet gestures around the room, to the windowless walls, to his legs. "It's -- no matter what I say it *is,* then I see it's the *oppo*site."

"Try."

"It's -- so cold it stings. Unbearable heat. White light, I cover my eyes. Suffocating dark. Reaching to hold. It grows so large it engulfs me. An opening I fall into. A closing up inside, my guts slamming against each other. If I could just touch it, then... it's intense gravity that pulls me down. It's weightlessness, I'm flying like blue tree vapors... "

Bullet has been staring at the light fixture on the infirmary ceiling. He closes his eyes and the reverse image goes green, then red, black outline quivering around it, yellow glowing at the edges.

"Blue tree vapors?"

◇   ◇

A silhouette, instant, brief shadow of the driver on the textured car ceiling, caused by the glove compartment light when Bullet, who is four, opens it to get the man his cigarettes. The taboo cellophane crinkle in his hands excites him, he inhales the adult smell of red plastic thermos coffee and smoke. Bullet fingers a blue plastic code ring in his corduroy pocket, watches out the car window for the blue tree ghosts. Lint tangled up around the ring. Pulls at it. Every mile or so a blue ghost glides across the road. Blue vapors, off into the trees. Bullet knows they're tree spirits, pulling up out of their roots, weightless. He falls asleep, his head against the cool metal of the jostling car door.

◇ ◇

Back in his cell, Bullet tries to envision his torso, his real torso, on the body of a paraplegic. Tries to see thin, white, useless legs like translucent fish fins. He tries to play the thing like a photo over his bed, but all that comes is interference of a photo of his true legs, tanned, haired and muscle-balled as his torso. Like those pencil drawings in "how to draw" books. The body constructed first of circles and then connected with arcs and lines, the circles erased. This is his body and he can't see it any other way.

tree bending sharply down

One night we came in from drinking. I hated it when we drank, I always lost control of how I wanted things to go with us. You passed out in my bed and I didn't want you there.

I sat on the edge of the tub, trying not to throw up. Swallowing fast, I forced myself to read a book to keep my mind off the dizziness from the wine. What was the book -- oh yes, that one about bonsais you gave me when you bought me the bonsai tree. It touched me when you gave me that, your way of trying to support my search for culture. Of course the tree died within a week. Plants always died in our place.

Then Carla came in with some hippie she'd met in the park. She wanted permission to go with him to Washington Island to pick cherries for the weekend. She was wearing my beaded belt wrapped around her fore-head and my turquoise ring. I couldn't bring myself to ask for them back, she looked so good in them. Her first beauty, not so gangling as before. And she had your blue eyes, only on a child's face they were so stark and intense, with knowledge a child shouldn't have. What was she then, twelve? And stoned and beer on her breath.

I didn't want her to go and she and I got into a fight. There was rawness between us that night; earlier she had found me crying in the kitchen about a love letter I'd found in your coat pocket.

'You let men devastate you too much,' she said. 'He's got all kinds of girls, don't you know that?'

I called her a bitch and told her not to give me advice 'til she was thirty. I felt bad about it but she angered me so, and I didn't want to hear about your other 'girls.'

'I'll never let a man do that to me!' she said, and flounced out with the hippie. She was proud of you, of your promiscuity. I couldn't stop her from going with the hippie. I slept on the sofa and in the morning when I told you where she'd gone, you shrugged and opened the refrigerator.

Bullet awoke remembering the blue tree vapors again. The silhouette on the car ceiling. Couldn't see the man's face. Who was it? He looked down. His cock was standing, remembering, under the sheet. Movement of the silhouette, hulk of a shoulder, arm, rapid movement. Bullet, a child waking up in a dark car. Something wrong. He stared out the car window into the dark blur of the trees rushing past. At that moment he understood how all movement was simultaneous -- the forward motion of the car, the receding motion of the landscape, and the motionless reflection of himself and the man in the window. Motionless except for the man's fingers on him, the thick forearm, pressing against the code ring in his pocket, pinching a nerve on Bullet's thigh. Bullet concentrated on not breathing, on catching the next vapor, the next escaping tree, not this. Not this coffee smell at first so pleasant and exciting like adventure, now turning in his throat, now wrong, heavy in his gut.

◇   ◇

Driving lessons. His daughter. Lenore had mentioned that in a letter, something about still having the photos from that day in the cemetery. That's where he took Carla sometimes when he and Lenore drove downstate for his visitation Sundays. Back when Carla was seven and he was paying the hundred a week. He took them to the cemetery out on that dirt road behind the school and let Carla drive between the tombstones and plastic rose wreaths, in whichever $250 El Dorado he was driving at the time. Carla giggled and screamed, even Lenore laughed and clutched the back of the seat. They had been happy that day; he had made them laugh. Both of them, his golden female cub, and his dark-haired Lenore, both of them all the time so pale, clenched jaws, the skin around their eyes so tight.

Somehow those driving lessons made it all right about the drive through blue vapors. That sensation before sleep, whatever it was, that thing that eluded him, wouldn't come for several nights after those visits with Carla.

After a few months living with Lenore, the sensation went away. It only came back when he was on the road, sleeping in the fruit-camp trailers. That's why he stayed on the road, away from her. So he could worry the thing, pick the scab, remember who he was.

Lenore has a bonsai now, in a rectangular blue tray on the hall table, next to the mail basket. She reads books on bonsai, reads their language as metaphor, as Zen. Last night she read, "If a limb once bent is immediately twisted in a different direction, cells will be ruptured and death will occur." When she mists and waters her bonsai, she talks to it, calls it "little woman." She's read that the impulse to bind tree roots in the Japanese was akin to the binding of the feet of Chinese women. Thinks of the Brazilian tribe in which each family keeps its adolescent girl hidden in a hut within the family hut, only letting her come out at night when no one will see her. Three years, so her skin will pale and make her more desirable.

Lenore thinks of how Bullet's skin will grow pale now, in

prison, like hers, like Carla's.

Lenore works at the Art Institute gift shop. Tut reproductions, unicorn posters, Hopper postcards, porcupine quill pouches, amethyst earrings. Since Bullet, her relationships are only with those at a distance. Sometimes lunch with a woman from the travel agency across the street, an occasional drink with the ineffable history professor, infrequent long distance calls to her mother, letters from Bullet in prison, the Green Assassin sometimes at the ICC stop. And, recently, the Underground Man.

The Underground Man lives in a condemned warehouse near the ICC tracks. The train Lenore takes home passes over the basement hole where he crawls in and out. She always sits on the left side so she can look down and see what he's having for dinner. Or if he has company. Or if it's full moon and he's pulled the cardboard box pieces in over the beaten-out doorhole, which means the air is too heavy, the blood moving too fast, dogs in packs. Those nights he curls in before sunset.

The Underground Man is the same man she's seen from a cab downtown two mornings in a row, walking fast like a child, as if someone has dressed him for school. Bright pink pants and a polyester jacket two sizes too large, with a worn elbow. His hair is combed up and greased into place, like 1953. As her cab passes he is watching the traffic anxiously, scanning the faces in the windows. They see each other. She looks away quickly, uneasy; his mind is much younger than hers, she sees that in his eyes.

The next morning there he is again, waiting to cross the same street. He turns, looks for her face. She lets their eyes connect. The cab stops for a light. The Underground Man kneels on his right knee, looks up to be certain Lenore is watching, then bends his head in concentration to untie his shoelace and tie it again. His fingers move so precisely that, from across the street, the wiry laces become vivid to her. He folds the left one into a loop before crossing it with the right, then pulls them tight. He does this well, shows her what he can do. The cab moves on.

Sometimes he has a friend at the warehouse, a brown bag
between them. They sit on their haunches, sucking cigarettes,
leaning against the warehouse, watching a can of soup on a stove
rack propped on two bricks. The Underground Man moves his
head emphatically as he talks into the soup. His friend listens
intently.

One full moon night she sees him crawling in. Leans out
on his elbow, pulls the cardboard door after him. Man from the
waist up, Goodwill polyester. From waist down underground
dweller, his legs damp and cold, sucking into the brown secret
earth floor.

For a whole week he is gone. The ride home doesn't feel
right those nights, she feels uneasy. Maybe she sees him waiting
in the morning at the blood donor center, putting his blood back
into the city flow. Maybe he is the one in dark glasses, his lean
jaws pulling on a cigarette, his clothes dusty from the belt down,
shoes wrinkled in mud.

tree with divided trunk

> ...a dream after you left, when you took up with the woman
> in Miami. She was showing me a photo of you in your life with
> her. Your eyes looked peaceful in an unfamiliar way. It was a
> view from above, as if you were on a ladder. I saw your hand
> fixing something, below you was a ditch with a hole in it. It
> seemed to be a positive picture of your new life. Then I realized
> that it was a picture of your head near the ground, and that your
> body was buried in sand, except your head... and it wasn't your
> hand at all but a very white, many fingered, feminine 'hand' that
> then became a large spider near your face. Then your eyes
> weren't peaceful, but showed fear and denial of fear...

He threw the letter to the floor, slapping the back of his hand
against the concrete wall next to the bed, again and again, in a
steady rhythm. It was all disturbing now. Her letters, her
dreams, his dreams, his legs. All these aches and aversions.

Not laughing now. Not crying either. Nowhere. Waiting. Just waiting.

She was right, it was like white spiders. He could see her dream vividly, as if it were his own. He understood it as his own; he read her letters as messages, clues. Yes, white spiders, that was good. That was how they made him feel, the women -- his ex, Carla, Lenore, the one in Miami, all of them. Touching, touching, warm hands, but then it became too much, too much friction on the skin, hands then too cool, white, slippery, shuddery.

Like with Carla, this summer on the road. He'd brought her back to her mother just in time. He'd taken her with him for the summer, travelling like she had three summers now. It wasn't kidnapping this time, now Carla was of age and had joined him on her own. But they didn't let her mother know where she was. The warrant.

It had been strained, this time. Carla was getting older. She'd taken a lover now and called him every few days. Bullet didn't like her calling, the calls might be traced. But he'd come around the corner from the men's room at a gas station and find her in a phone booth, wiggling her leg against the leg holding her up, twisting the phone cord around her fingers.

It wasn't just her calling that bothered him. It was the way men looked at her in the truck stops, and how that blue vapor feeling came now, even when Bullet was wide awake, every time Carla poured him coffee from the thermos. In the motels he let her talk to him in the dark, side by side on the bed, until she passed out. He'd stay there, nodding, grunting assents, watching the shadow of his arm gigantic above the bed, moving the cigarette back and forth to his lips.

Once she fell asleep, he'd get up and spread a blanket on the floor and sleep there, next to the bed. She never asked about it in the morning.

Bullet told her he'd bring her back to her mother at the end of the summer. She was angry, wanted to stay with him, go pick fruit in Florida. But he insisted her life be as normal as possible. He would be her only contact with streetlife. That's how he felt when he was sober. When he drank, he let go, he laughed, he patted her ass real hard when she danced by with the cowboys. But he always took her back with him to their motel room after. He never let her go with them. He'd figured he'd get caught when he showed his face, taking her back home. Seven year warrant. He'd never get out of town. That was how it would be. But he'd take the chance, because if he went back to Florida, he was going alone. There he would be free of that sensation his child unwittingly caused in him. He didn't want her there in the mornings, dressing with him before daylight, didn't want her giggles adding to the crashing of the ladders into the gothic silence of the grapefruit grove, the rungs tearing back the overnight webs of the crab spiders which glistened from tree to tree. That was his time, his alone, without the women. Just his own sweat.

tree with roots embracing rock

Lenore reads Bullet's letter in the hall, then stands staring into the bonsai tree. She picks up the bottle to mist its leaves, rearranges the rocks.

Nothing below the waist has feeling now. For several weeks. I'm not really worried, though. I watch it all like a movie. Because, every morning, although I can't feel a thing, my cock stands high. I'll name that sensation. It's just a matter of time.

She dreams it is the end of the world. She is in the front seat of a thick, glass train carrying the survivors down into the earth. The train pushes through brown walls and skeletal fences, crushing them, moving them aside. The end of the world has left all surfaces soft like wet crackers. There is no impact. The train stops in the warehouse, lets her off to wait there for the end. The Underground Man, covered with cankers, is dumped in a gunny sack next to her. He is barely conscious, but his mouth clamps onto her breast through her shirt as he falls. They are being left to die by starvation. She calls out to the train as it moves on, calls out, "Wait! I don't belong here! This man is dying, diseased, there's been some mistake."

"There's been no mistake," a voice calls back from the train.

"OK," she says, "I just wanted to make sure."

She pulls the man's mouth -- is it the Underground Man? Is it Bullet? -- from her nipple, pushes his limp body aside. She sits down to wait. Crawls to the remains of the doorhole after the train passes through, pulls in the pieces of crushed cardboard. They hardly cover the hole anymore, the train has widened it. She drapes gunny sacks to cover the cracks. Almost total dark now. His rasping breath is a steady, comforting sound. She huddles into herself. Pleased by the smell of wet earth cracking into her nostrils as she pushes her feet deep into the ground.

◇ ◇

The morning after Lenore's dream, Bullet awakes to the awareness that his legs are back, sweating under the rough blanket, the toes sticking to each other. Wet heaviness when he moves them, as if they are impacted in thick mud.

◇ ◇

It is spring. Lenore airs out the rooms in the morning and leaves the windows open when she leaves the apartment.

When she returns in the evening, she mists and waters her "little woman." Leaning into the little tree, she closes her eyes, and inhales deeply the familiar smell of wet earth. Smiling, puzzled at some memory that tugs momentarily, but will not surface, she picks a small white spider off the rim of the blue planter.

Where We've Come Strangers

It's three in the morning in your new apartment. Your lights are on because you don't want the world to know you are vulnerably asleep. The doorbell rings, you wake in a dream, look out the window, is it the former tenant? It looks like her, then you realize you never met the former tenant, only heard her voice once on the phone when you called about changing the utilities. It's a stranger at the door, she smiles at you through the window like embarrassment or recognition, you look out puzzled. It's a girl, so small at 3:00 a.m. She asks to come in and use your phone. You say sure, sure, uh huh, uh huh, tell me the number, I don't know you, tell me the number, I don't know you, I'll call for you, is that Ok, is that Ok?

She says sure, thanks, says a number. How convenient it all is, just like a dream, that the phone and the window and the door are so close. She watches you through the curtain dial the number tell her sister to come get her. Her sister is asleep, wants to know who you are, why are you calling, where is her sister, is her boyfriend with her? Ahah, you think, that's it, he's out there crouching behind the bushes, this is one of those... you ask through the window, is your boyfriend with you? she looks over her shoulder, she says no, she doesn't say it but somehow you know they had a fight, he pushed her out the car, he drove away, she saw your light,

158

your up-all-night light, a beacon in the dark, she came to your light... you tell her sister to meet her at the station on 8th Street. She hangs up, in a hurry, hurrying down already. You wonder what part of town she lives in, how fast will she get there.

The girl says thanks and leaves. You just pulled the covers over you when there's a knock at the door. It's her again, she wants to know how far to the station at 8th, which way to get there, can she get there by these back streets? No, you keep saying, I don't think so, you have to go by Central, that's the only way I know, it's all a blur, she goes off into the night, looks confused, you pull the covers back over you. Then you realize she is in danger, she can't go all that way alone in the dark at 3:00 a.m. in this neighborhood, but she's gone, which way? Where? Should you dress, run out, run up and down streets calling... what was her name? You remember a name but was it her name or her sister's name? You don't sleep the rest of the night trying trying trying to remember her name her sister's name her name...

In your memory you asked her in, you said like a mother or an aunt you can't run all that way it's dangerous out there, here come in, call your sister back, tell her my address, I'll make some tea, we'll sit here uncomfortably waiting for her,2 I'll ask you what happened, why are you out alone at 3:00 a.m., where is your boyfriend, what is all this about and why why why did you pick me, pick my door, my light, why don't you look afraid, if I were you I'd be terrified, would you like some more tea?

And you want to run an ad the next day, *To the young woman who knocked on my door to use the phone at 3:00 a.m., did you get home all right? Did your sister find you Ok? Are you all right? Are you all right?*

Sometimes in the middle
of something like pouring boiling water over coffee grounds or
checking the mail box or finding notes to yourself you realize
you are still trying to remember her name her sister's name her
name...

Water Rites

Before she came to the desert she read of lovers here, their tough reptilian skin, their boots, their sparse rooms with bones, their pistol-packing way of loving. She envisioned that desert expanse which would disperse a man's coyote cries from dust-gritted sheets. She envisioned her pinon-scented hair tangling over the edge of the bed as she watched the scorpion's tail feathering a talc trail across the blood-pigmented floor.

She finds a sculptor who has become the thirst of this place. His mud room studio of cobwebs, stacked cattle skulls, white and bronze geometric forms -- his papers rattle like snake skeletons when the wind comes through the heavy two-hundred-year-old door carved "Jimenez". But he is not Jimenez, his eyes are that Mediterranean blue like her metal courtyard chairs, like the trim which chips from her cranked window frame. He is Anglo, a west coast seed tenaciously rooted, choking out the insidious weeds. The realtors have built a condo behind his kitchen, dug a ditch outside his door, have warehoused his alley, declared him a commercial zone. But he stays ten years, his adobe now past congruity, and starts each day with thick, black tea. The sun rips through the holes of the Navajo rug at the window by his bed, forming white bandage strips of heat along his arms as he lies sketching last night's dream in geometric forms on yellow pages. He stays.

161

Restless in her place on the back side of the mountain, she sweeps out the dust of insect shells, cactus, lime peelings, rusted nails of ancient wheels, jars of blessed Chimayo chapel dirt, skins of chiles. She wants to start clean again, back east, twelve stories high, like the architecture magazines: clerestory windows, skylight white with ebony trim, expanse of polished floor -- oak or marble -- scattered *New York Times,* just one piece on a pedestal (perhaps O'Keeffe, the late black sculpted egg), cubes of chrome, seats of mauve. This redbrownpink mud wall wearies her where the rain stains in slow drying brown patches.

From the plaza balcony she watches an old Hopi woman who squats, sullen in her wine, lifts her sunset orange skirts and pees into the curb as if it were the mesa. A native with the native's disregard. Precious liquid -- wine, piss, water. How can they miss what they have never known? She watches the woman's water shrink on hot tar. She sips her hotel drink. Too much margarita salt.

Remembers ocean salt on her upper lip, how her hair was fuller back there. She has not forgotten sea level. Maybe it is time to leave. Back to something green and wet, no more water sorrow, some humidity between her skin and the cartilage which holds it stretched just so.

No. She's not going anywhere. There is this man to be resolved, the alchemy of his scent. The sun's heat brings it up to her when he stands near on the mesa, his lips cracked, his words sticking to the roof of his mouth. By chance she has touched the skin under his shirt tail, along his spine, and it is silk is roses is oiled skin of newborn. She wishes to browse his body -- the taste of salt on his neck, his hands acrid with foundry metal. But he is not easy, he has not touched a woman in years. This and these scents pull her to his door. To his shards and puzzles and dark brow, his mouth a twist of lime, his eyes that same blue as the sky which moves over his roof, over his yard piled with cattle thigh and pelvic bone. His soft voice cracks dry, his hair has grown more grey each time she comes to him.

Conversations each midnight across the mountain, lights blown out at both ends of the wire: "Everyone here is so self-sufficient, standing apart like dark spiny shapes in the desert," she sighs into the lightweight black princess phone receiver.

"Look around you, lady, everything is in motion," he laughs.

"Are you in motion?" she asks, staring at the telephone receiver which has grown heavy in her hand. It is now deco, black. When did it change?

"If you stand a certain distance from me and I walk with my eyes closed and feel my hands on your hair, then I know I am," he answers.

"I envisioned your breast," he whispers. She jiggles the receiver, the phone has now become a wooden box on the wall. There is no time to question this, there are metal parts she must press to her ear. "Speak louder," she cries, "The mountain stands between us."

"Your breast," he repeats. "I -- "

"Does this mean you want to touch me?" she asks.

"It means I already have," he sighs. He has learned the inevitability of seasons, the saguaro drinks itself for only so long.

"*This* is my breast," she says, opening her blouse to him on the ground in the moon. For once, she wants to withhold nothing. She cries out and lets him suckle her up to, into and past the pain. His tongue and teeth move deep and hard and bring up milk that was never there, urge all her body liquids high. The ground beneath her clothes runs wet, the sand grows white with mammary foam.

After, on the desert that was beach, she lies skeletal, bleached. She has lain there for centuries; she is the clacking sound of vertebrae, of the rattler's tail. The wind whistles between her joints. "Is this what you wanted?" he laughs, now in motion. "Is this why you came?"

Afterword

Harry says he needs something light for this collection. It's so serious about men and women, things aren't all bad, you know.

I don't know, I say, I just don't know.

Try, he says.

Well, there was this guy once and this woman who thought she was, you know, feeling things, and it had been a while and she was scared but he made her laugh and...

That sounds like a story to me, says Harry. Sure does, says Adela. We click our truth-serum margaritas and I linger in their love, their having-found, their humor, how Adela takes Harry in to play *Upwords®* to get his mind off the wicker patch, the computer glitch, WIPP...

◇ ◇

I will tell you a bedtime story, then, about sleeping with a wild horse, but you have to remember it's light.

Very

very

light.

◇ ◇

165

On Sleeping with the Wild Horse

It had been a long time. Elise had been sleeping alone on the left side for years. In the morning she turned back the covers on the left, the right stayed unwrinkled, untouched. Something told her, "If you take up the whole bed, no one will come."

So, the morning after he came to her bed, she was afraid.

To get in touch with her feelings she sat on the rug, cross-legged, courtyard door open, closed her eyes and her lower self (LS) and her higher self (HS) had a talk:

HS: Why are you afraid?

LS: Because he slept barricaded, against the wall, put one pillow under his head, one over his head, one he held to his chest, one at his feet, one between us, I reached in to find him, he wasn't there. "I love this bed," his voice echoed from the depths of his pillow cave. And then he slept.

HS: So?

LS: So, I was restless all night, I've read the how-to-love books, I know what sleeping patterns forebode... and I know how lovely he looks when he's walking away, in a cafe, on the sidewalk to his car, out my door through the grass -- he is a horse, a sleek, dark horse. I have discovered one of his best moves is walking away.

HS: And you're afraid that is the last trick he will show you.

166

LS: Right.

HS: You act as if sleeping together were an act of war. It is not so. It is love, connecting, the honey, to do so with each other is an expression of trust, the beginning of the run, not the end. Good lord, woman, just let the mind and emotions run their course, they always do. He seeks solace and warmth, so do you. Choose love, not fear. By the way, you're late for work.

The house sat on Native American burial land, the archaeologists said. Large, low, made of mud, filled with shadow and light, laced with grapes, hunkered down amid fruit and willow and cottonwood trees, visited by toads and moths and roadrunners and bats and the annual nests of baby sparrows under the eaves. Elise and her housemates knew an old woman had lived and died in the house years ago. They had found some of her things in the cabinets and closets and put them to use -- books, quilts, cast iron pots. They had seen and sensed her ghost, she chanted and moaned all night in the walls, she closed their windows, remembered to turn on the night light, fed and brushed the cats when they forgot and shook her head, tskk!ing, wondering why they were all so single in the house.

He passed the test, he loved the house. So many others had come there and had not seen the house, had not understood, had just taken what they wanted or taken nothing at all and never returned.

"If you think it's an unfair test," Elise told her friends, "Consider: if a man can't see the house, he can't see anything, he's not awake. There is a certain aliveness I require. He has to understand the house, that's first."

And he did, he took it all in, he knelt inside of it, he spread out his arms across the adobes, he breathed deeply, he understood. Only moments later Elise smelled brownies baking. The old woman approved. "Finally!" she said, shaking her head and wiping flour on her apron.

And then the cats, that helped if you took to the cats.

Only first it was the cats that took to him.

The bruiser, the bully cat, the one who growled and disdained humankind -- Elise found him curled in the man's lap, clenching the man's torso with claws, *Not going to move*, he purred, because the man was laughing and stroking his fur with a white candlestick. Astonished, Elise watched, thinking, of course, *You can stroke me with that candlestick anytime!*

This man was very much alive.

"Is he coming back?" her housemates asked when the man left. "It feels so... fertile... having him around. Hope he comes back."

He was a horse who found the gate who entered the yard who ate the apples who eyed the door who stayed a while.

In a weathered old book of country wisdom, left by the old woman of the house, Elise found a chapter entitled *Country Rules for Wild Horses Entering Your Yard:*

1. Leave food and water, but not too close to the house.

2. Be very quiet.

3. Watch from the door.

4. Move very slowly.

5. If the horse leaves, leave the gate open and go about your business, don't wait by the window.

6. When the horse comes back, let it approach you for touching. Later, for riding. Don't take these liberties for granted.

7. Keep the food and water fresh. It's a ritual, respect it.

8. Don't forget: animals sense your fear. Keep the psychic channels open.

9. Be gentle: this is a fragile moment.

He had fallen deeply into the pillows where Elise could not reach him. She tried to find his fingers, he could not open his fist, she felt so afraid sleeping cold and alone at the edge of his pillow cave. In the morning she left the bed before he woke, hurt, scared, thinking, *You will not do this to me, you man, you will NOT!*

Instead, he called out, "Come 'ere," like a sulking boy and of course she came back to the bed. He turned away again, his back to her, and pulled her close around him, holding her hand against his chest and they slept another hour. Before they fell asleep, he whispered, "This is the part I don't get at home in my bed."

Elise begin to understand his need. And about the pillows. They were not a barricade. They were something like the packing of wounds.

The next time he slept with her, she was ready, thinking about his beauty, about the honey, thinking about the word "tenderness." And thinking about another friend who taught her how they could be sand box children together, a better way than men and women at war...

After loving he turned to the wall again. Elise placed the pillows carefully, one at his head, one at his feet, one at his chest (but not one between them) and told him, "Seeing as how you like my pillows so much," and, surprised, he said, "*Thank you.*" Like he really meant it. He took her by the hand, pulled her close around him again, this time all night, her hand reached through the pillows, found his fingers, his chest, his sweat and heat and dreams and the place where his heart was torn and they held their hands over that place all night sleeping together down in the pillow cave.

And all night a smile never ever left her face.

He slept like a wild horse and Elise rode him without falling. In the morning the sheets were rolled down to naked mattress, pillows crushed against the wall, covers on the floor. Warily, the cat crawled out from under, eyeing the beast. Before the man left, he climbed over the bed, tucked in corners, reassembled the linen, laughing the whole time. Put the pillows back in a row. "Sure do like this bed," he said, smoothing the wrinkles from the old woman's quilt.

Fresh food and water. What did horses eat? Apples and hay and honey. In the morning Elise left these by the bed for him.

She watched him leave, his tail flicked, his long legs carried his prance out her gate, his head danced to the side, his dark mane shining, she saw his eyes from the side staring into the trees into the ditch into the sun. He paused, fingering the bruises along his flanks. They felt good. He liked it here, he liked the house and the pillows and the lady. She could tell.

"Will that one be coming back?" her housemates asked, watching from the window.

"Get away from the window," Elise said, smiling and thinking about Rule #9 on her way back to her room to clean up the hay and apple cores from his feeding.

MORE WOMEN'S WRITING
FROM AMADOR PUBLISHERS

EVA'S WAR:
A TRUE STORY OF SURVIVAL
by Eva Krutein

ISBN: 0-938513-09-5 [Trade $17]
ISBN: 0-938513-08-7 [Paper $9]
260 pp.

This gripping story of flight, refugees, privation, defeat, moral quandaries, growth and finally healing is strangely moving and compelling. It becomes a powerful anti-war statement from a woman's perspective. One year is recounted, beginning in January, 1945. Danzig, a Free City between the Great Wars, was seized by Hitler in 1939, and threatened by Soviet troops as Eva flees with her daughter.

They say that history is written by the winners, yet this bit of history comes from that nation which lost the war. Now that that nation is recovered and reunited, this sort of remembering is all the more important. And Eva Krutein is no loser. She and her family emigrated to Chile, and then to California, where they now live. She is an accomplished musician and writer.

"A marvelously moving and often humorous real-life story... sad revelations, painful memories, excruciating experiences are tempered by compassion, love and a powerful, contagious optimism. Music permeates this tale." Alfred-Maurice de Zayas, JD, PhD, Senior Legal Officer, The United Nations, Geneva, Switzerland

"Her novel-like presentation makes for exciting reading. The story of German refugees has not been well covered, so this should find a place in academic and public libraries." -- THE LIBRARY JOURNAL

"An excellent, provocative and important book." -- Laurel Speer, poet and critic

"Eva's account is one of fervent desire for peace in a setting of chaos, deprivation and horror... Yet EVA'S WAR is not exclusively about grief and guilt. It is about forgiveness, trust, accomplishment and love of life." -- Thora Guinn, ALBUQUERQUE PEACE CENTER NEWS

THE TIME DANCER:
A NOVEL OF GYPSY MAGIC
by Zelda Leah Gatuskin

ISBN: 0-938513-12-5 [245 pp. Paper $10]
A romantic tale of time travel, mistaken identities and parallel worlds. Can one really navigate the sea of time? When George Drumm falls in love with the Gypsy Esmarelda, he must learn the secrets of the Spiral Map of Time, or lose her to the future. But the Gypsy is on her own quest. The two leapfrog across the Spiral in search of lost cats, missing satchels and each other, and in the process share glimpses of their magical universe with the residents of the dusty town of Caliente, in the Alternate World.

Novelist and mixed media artist, Zelda Leah Gatuskin, resides in Albuquerque, NM. THE TIME DANCER draws on her work with mandalas and symbols as well as her study of ethnic dance.

"A twisted, clever, spellbinding tale for the 1990's. Gatuskin creates a vivid and bizarre universe, certain to satisfy the appetite of enthusiasts of such authors as Lewis Carroll and J.R.R.Tolkein. "
-- Michael Bush, Associate Artistic Director
MANHATTAN THEATRE CLUB, New York City

"Gatuskin weaves a delightfully magical story, which tricked me into thinking she was from another time, or maybe a Gypsy in a past life. I'll never look at my cats the same again. "
-- Lisa Law, author, photographer, producer, director
FLASHING ON THE SIXTIES

"THE TIME DANCER is a delightful story -- full of quest, high spirits, memorable characters and thought-provoking ideas. Gatuskin takes an intricate premise, time travel, and makes it clear, believable and focused. "
-- Suzanne K. Pitré, playwright and author

"I am intrigued. I find particularly fascinating her use of certain shapes to travel time, since these shapes are the foundation of this deeply spiritual dance form. As a teacher of Belly Dance and its esoteric significance, I would highly recommend that my students read this magical tale. "
-- Swari Hhan, author
BEYOND THE EROTICISM OF BELLY DANCE:
BELLY DANCE AS SACRED DANCE

ALSO THESE NOVELS, FROM MEN'S "FEMININE SIDE"

THE HUMMINGBIRD BRIGADE: A NOVEL OF HEALING
by D. L. Condit

ISBN: 0-938513-05-2 [165 pp. Paper $8] Each member of a tragi-comic quartet rebounds from personal loss and pain with a shared resolve to break the chain of abuse and persevere gracefully in the face of adversity and injustice. Brilliant barbs of satire are softened by sensitivity to suffering, especially of the young. The action moves from New Jersey to New Mexico, and celebrates the healing power of the Land of Enchantment.

A therapist specializing in troubled children and their families, Condit is an accomplished, published poet.

"Breathing the air of that much-abused, exquisitely painful era, the pre-mythological Sixties... Only a few things matter: love and caring, and not killing people for bad reasons. --THE WILDERNESS OUTLOOK, Silver City, NM

"Insight...about life, the young of today and what they fear... Condit has brought forth in his own poetic style those usually guarded emotions we are too frightened to look at ourselves, or to share with another." -- THE TAOS NEWS

"The book has a gentle, delicate quality about it, even as it describes some very harsh realities." -- CHIRON REVIEW

"...introduces us to some sensitive vulnerable individuals who alight upon a society more than willing to h ave them cozy up to injustice, intolerance, violence and death. So there is a very real need to deal with loss."
-- Saffron Rice-Field, Santa Fe

"Confusion, contradiction, disguised hope and ultimate triumph and exhilaration: this book is for people who will always remain in touch with the child in their heart."
-- Craig Waggoner, JOURNAL OF CHILD AND YOUTH CARE WORK

SOULS AND CELLS REMEMBER:
A LOVE STORY
by H. G. Z. Willson

ISBN: 0-938513-03-6 [188 pp. $8]

a tender love story
full of anger and ancient longings,
cultural/racial confrontation
and reincarnation,
moving in place
from New Mexico to the Susquehanna,
and in time
from the present to the 1750's
and back...

Willson's characters are global and cosmic travelers, so true to their belief in peace and the power of love, that they easily become the reader's own friends, teachers and lovers, with voices that echo long after the story has been read. They shine with a refreshing honesty, while they fight to understand the workings of their deepest psychic selves.

"Journeying across the continent from West to East and across two centuries in time, protagonists Thomas Grady and Flora Esperante confront ancestral images, hostility, sex, outward anger and inner reality. According to my friends who know, the white teacher and the Native American potter accurately introduce readers to the fascinating realm of metaphysics." -- BOOKS OF THE SOUTHWEST

"...a story of love and reincarnation. An interesting tale, and Willson carries it off well. ...Thomas and Flora explore racism, sex, family ties, metaphysics and history -- but the tone does not come across as didactic. Rather the love story [which proves to span several centuries] is primary. ... A pleasant and different read." -- FACT SHEET FIVE

"Questions of race and identity turn out to be a gateway to a deeper human sharing." -- Uncle River, THE MOGOLLON NEWS

"This book is about prejudice -- and it's true! I loved the Indian woman." -- THE PLACITAS READER

"A dream you would like to have come true for yourself." -- Silver Ravenwolf

THE SPIRIT THAT WANTS ME:
A NEW MEXICO ANTHOLOGY
Edited by J. Dianne Duff, Jill Kiefer, & Michelle Miller

ISBN: 1-879272-00-8 [Paper $19.95] 401 pp.

"...I can't tell you what it is. It's a spirit... It's here, in this landscape ...It's something to do with wild America. And it's something to do with me... Now I am where I want to be: with the spirit that wants me." **D. H. Lawrence, *St. Mawr***

"Do you have something to say about why you live in New Mexico?..." That was the first line of a flier we distributed around the state. Our question was directed to residents who had not been born in New Mexico. The flier, along with press releases, word-of-mouth networks and personal letters, brought us over one thousand pages of material. Each story, however personal, shared the theme of a unique aura that, despite various hardships, makes it preferable to be alive here than to be alive elsewhere." **-- THE EDITORS**

"If there is magic in this volume -- small wonder. Whether they're pipefitters, pastry chefs or poets, these *extranjeros* born again as New Mexicans have been touched by magic, and in these sparkling pages they have passed it on in letters, journals, poetry and prose..."
-- from the Foreword, **Norman Zollinger**
Golden Spur Award Winner, Western Writers of America

"*The contributors include poets, accountants, professors, farmers, painters, lawyers, therapists, carpenters, folksingers, librarians. The are young, middle-aged or old; they've been in New Mexico one year, seven years, thirty years. They write at length, or a few lines, of the circumstances that brought them to Albuquerque, Clovis, Española, Farmington, Las Cruces, Santa Fe, Silver City, Taos and a dozen other towns. They speak, too, about the difficulties of life in New Mexico and the gifts that make it all worthwhile.*" **-- NEW MEXICO MAGAZINE**

"*...A book that can offer enjoyable reading for all residents of New Mexico, whether transplants who might like to compare notes, or natives seeking insight on just what these people are doing here. Non-residents can read it to see what they're missing. The many and diverse segments that comprise it not only reflect the character of the state itself, but make it one of those books that a reader can put down and pick up again and again, opening it at random to find some new gem each time.*" **-- SEEN FROM SPACE**